Kassondra 2

D ALAN PAULY

KASSONDRA 2

iUniverse books may be ordered through booksellers or by contacting:

iUniverse
1663 Liberty Drive
Bloomington, IN 47403
www.iuniverse.com
1-800-Authors (1-800-288-4677)

ISBN: 978-1-5320-6952-9 (sc)
ISBN: 978-1-5320-6953-6 (e)

Print information available on the last page.

iUniverse rev. date: 02/28/2019

Plot Synopsis

The destiny of a person is connected not only with
those things he, himself, created and does, but also with
what happened to his soul in previous incarnations.
...One's existence is therefore continuity, the
sustaining of a certain fundamental rise to the
surface which does not seem to belong to the present.

-Rabbi Steinsaltz-

Rebecca Marshall is a widowed mother of two, living in a small town in Colorado. Her major concern is getting through another day financially and emotionally intact with her two children.

But centuries away, in a primitive country besieged by an evil curse, forces are at work to draw Rebecca back to her destiny...a destiny that has followed her through countless incarnations and is now demanding to be fulfilled.

Rebecca is taken back through time to the period when she was a woman warrior in the country of Ektarr, called Kassondra. She was the only person who could slay the Beast, a feat in which she succeeded admirably.

However, she discovered that there are other personifications of the evil wizard's curse with which she must deal before she can face the wizard, himself, in the ultimate battle of good versus evil.

Every weapon known to man had been used to destroy the Dragon, but all had failed.

His mysterious ability to withstand bullets and explosives was baffling and frightening.

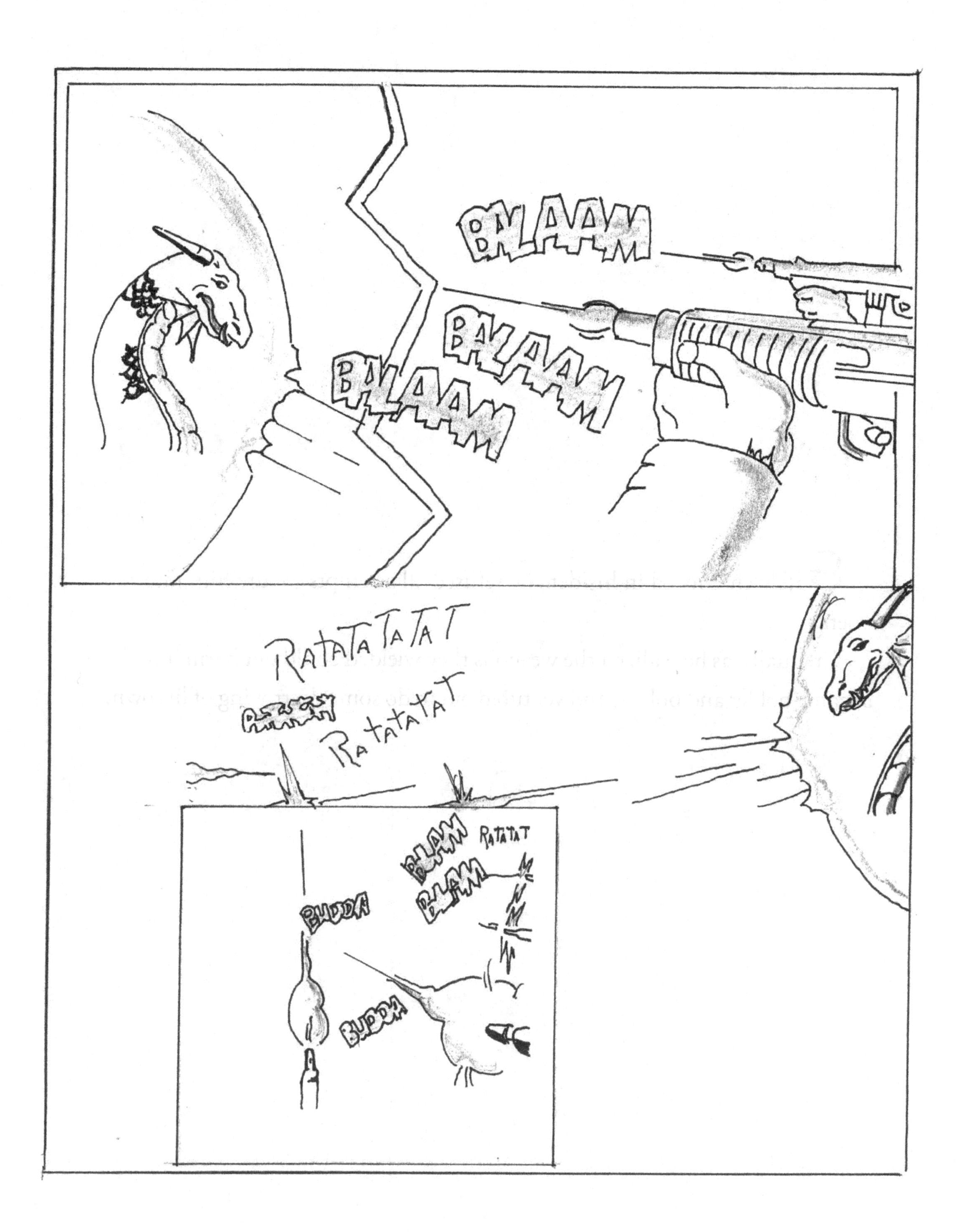
BALAAM
BALAAM
BALAAM
RATATATATAT
RATATATAT
BLAM
RATATAT
BLAM
BUDDA
BUDDA

Safely ensconced in his den, he refused all attempts to lure him into the open.

Gradually, as he realized the weapons they wielded could not harm him, he became bolder and bolder, and ventured out to do some destroying of his own.

Dragon
Come out

Come out
Dragon

Dragon

Dragon, Dragon

Dragon Dragon
Dragon
Dragon
Drag

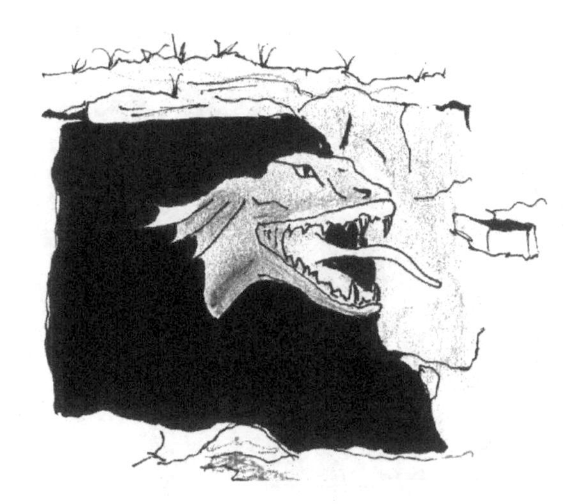

Kassondra approached with her mystical sword.

"Let's do this, Dragon!" she shouted. Confused as to why nothing seemed to harm him she hoped against hope that the sword that had saved her before would work again.

The Dragon circled her mockingly.

"Let's dance, Kassondra! Who holds the mightier weapon? Is it my tail or your sword?"

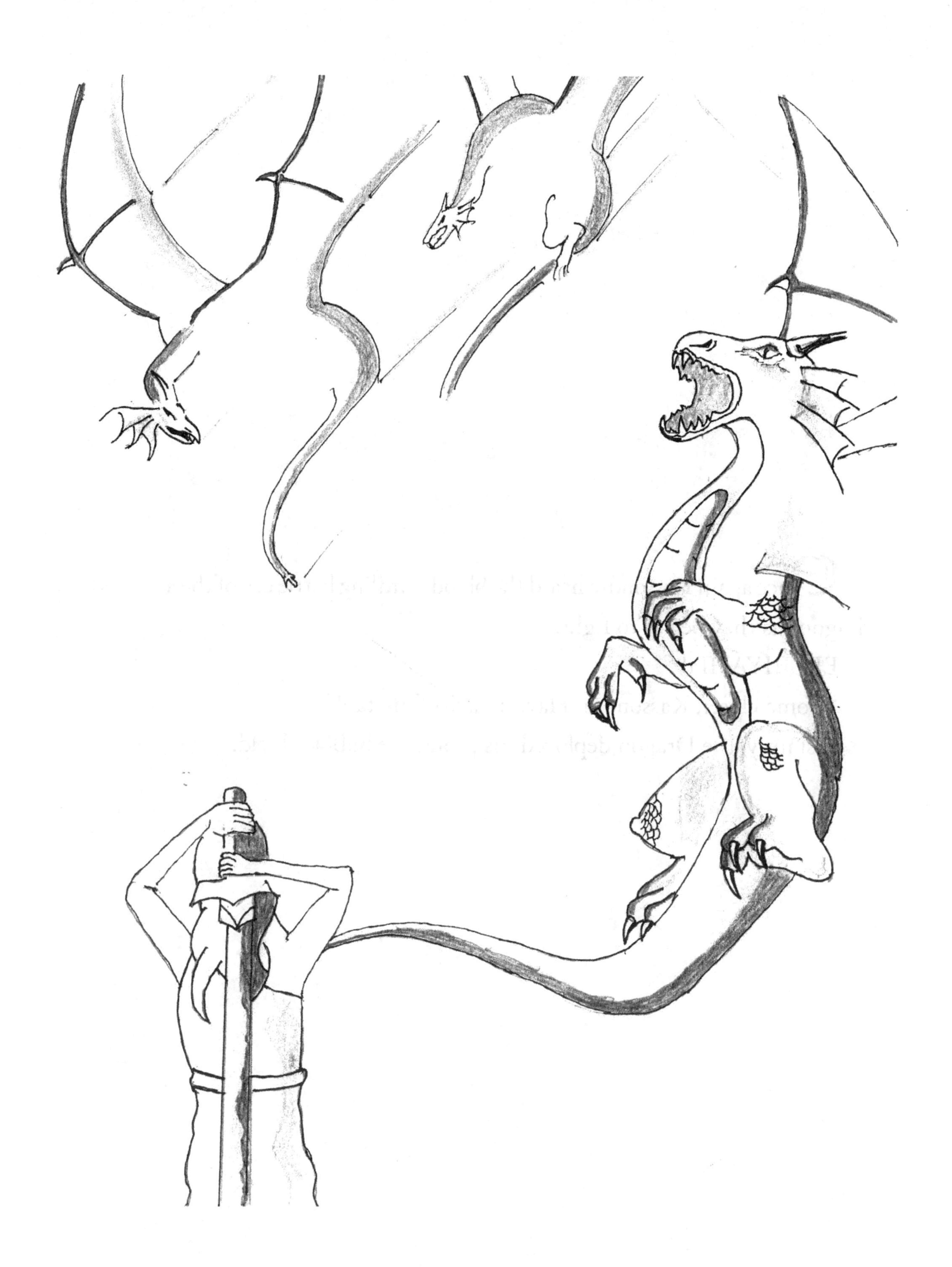

Once again Kassondra heard the blood-curdling battle cry of the accursed dragons as they began to fight.

EEEIIIYAHH!

"Come closer, Kassondra. Have a taste of my tail!"

Instantly, the Dragon deployed his protective bubble shield.

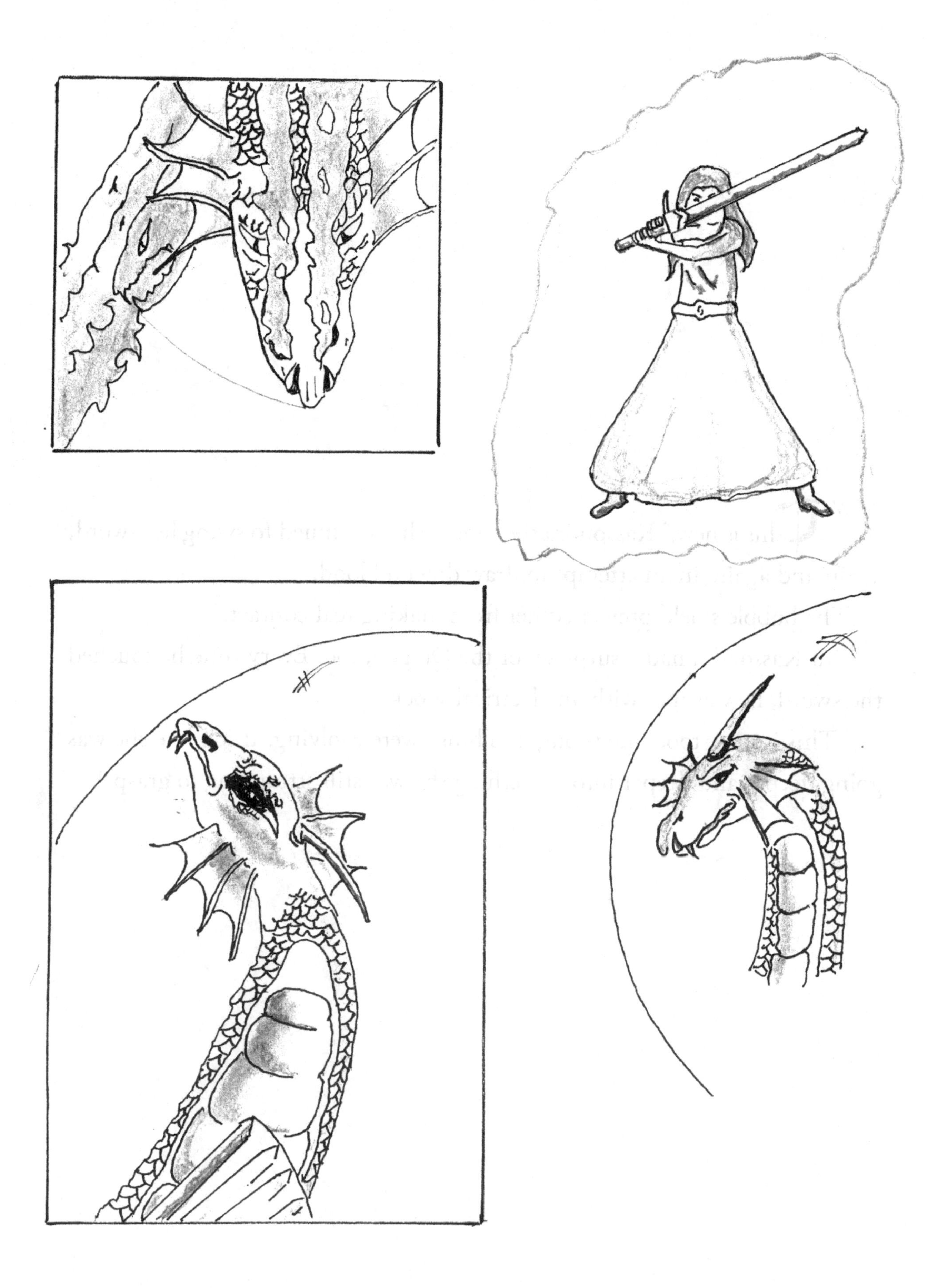

"This is new," Kassondra thought as she continued to swing her sword, again and again, in an attempt to draw dragon blood.

The bubble shield prevented her from making real contact.

But Kassondra had a surprise for the Dragon, too. Every time he touched the sword, he was met with an electrical shock.

"This is new, too," she thought. Things were evolving. It felt like she was going deeper and deeper into something she was still struggling to grasp.

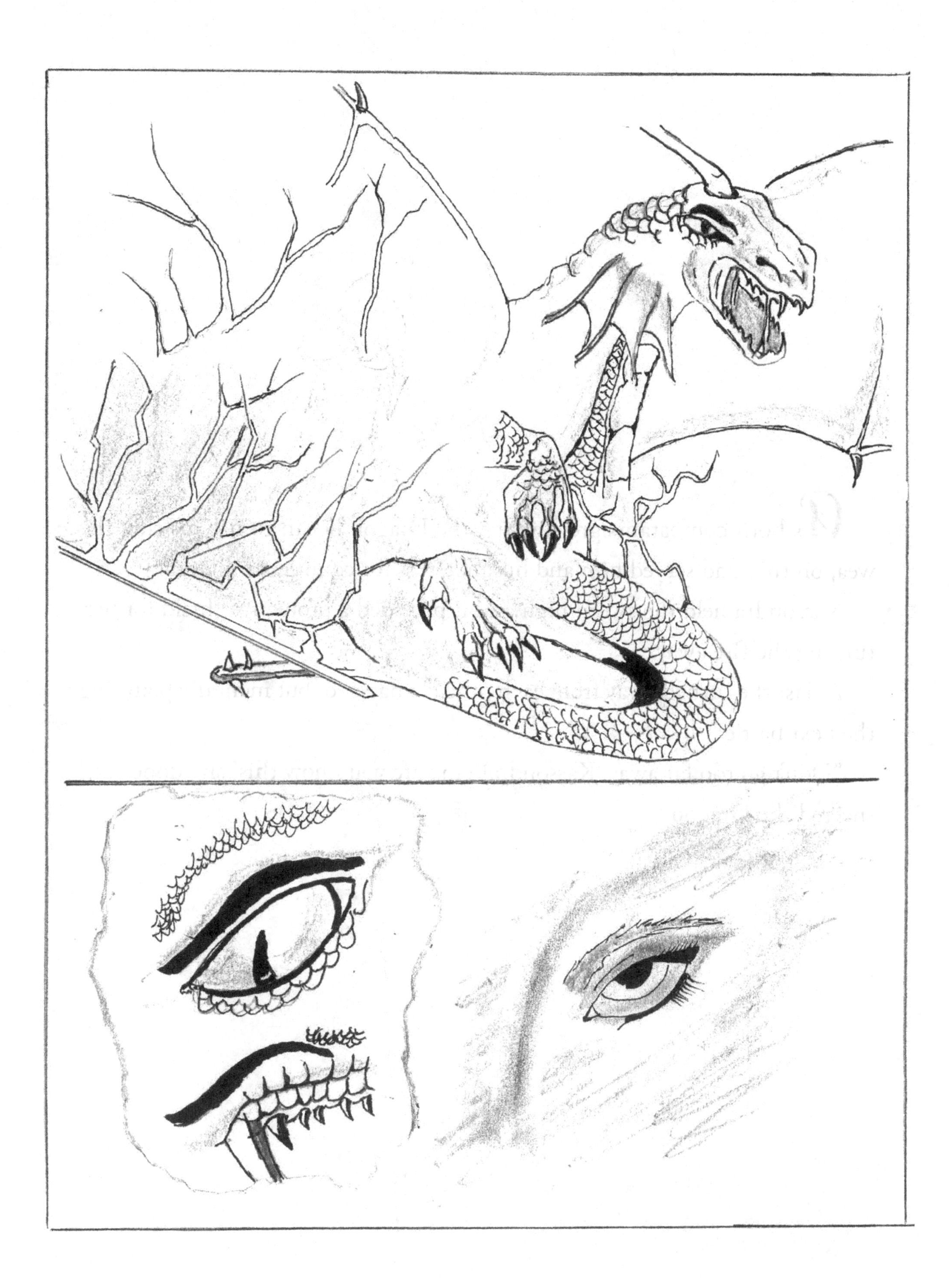

As both combatants grew weary, the Dragon began to use his fire, the weapon that had served him and his ancestors for countless millennia.

Kassondra held the sword high and it provided a protective shield for her, turning the fire away.

At last the turned away from each other, exhausted, but mentally planning the next battle.

"Don't go too far away, Kassondra! I'm sure you know this isn't done yet," sneered the Dragon.

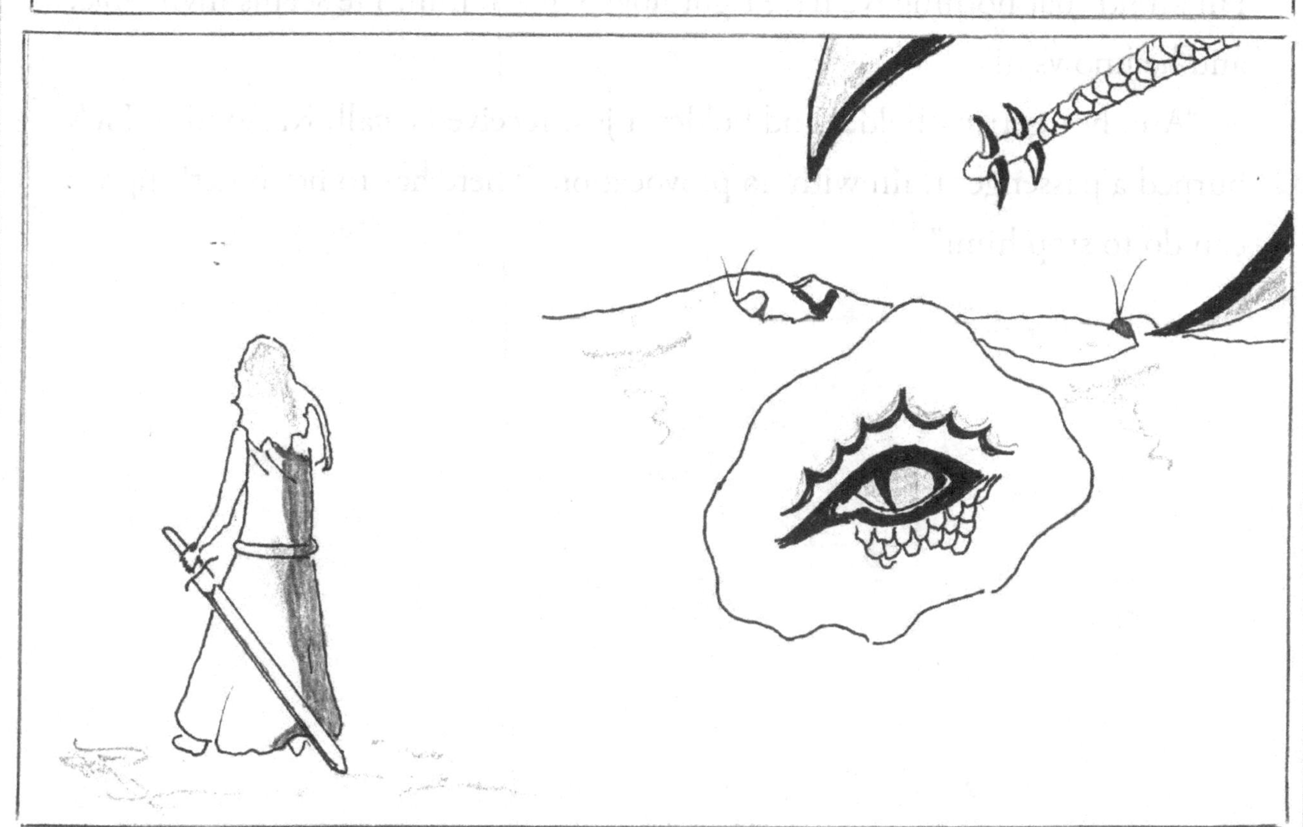

Needing to talk to someone and feel connected to her "real" life, Kassondra once again turns to Mayor Johnson.

"He has some kind of protective bubble that I'm not familiar with, Mayor. I'm afraid that nothing we have right now will kill him. He seems invincible, and he knows it!"

"And he's getting bolder and bolder. I just received a call, Kassondra. He's burned a passenger train with no provocation. There has to be something we can do to stop him!"

MEAN WHILE
Ring Ring Ring

The Dragon, leaving the smoldering train and its cargo of dead humans, flies over a military base and is spotted by an air traffic controller.

"Colonel, it's in our airspace! It's flying low and, God, it's huge!"

"Damn! Will nothing do this bastard in!?! I need my two best men in the air, stat! Get me Captain Allen and Lt. Mike.

NOW!"

"How quaint. They tried planes once before...and FAILED. Bring it on, boys! I've got my eye on both of you!"

"LT. MIKE! I've got a visual! Do you see him?" "Not yet, Captain! ...OH MY GOD!"

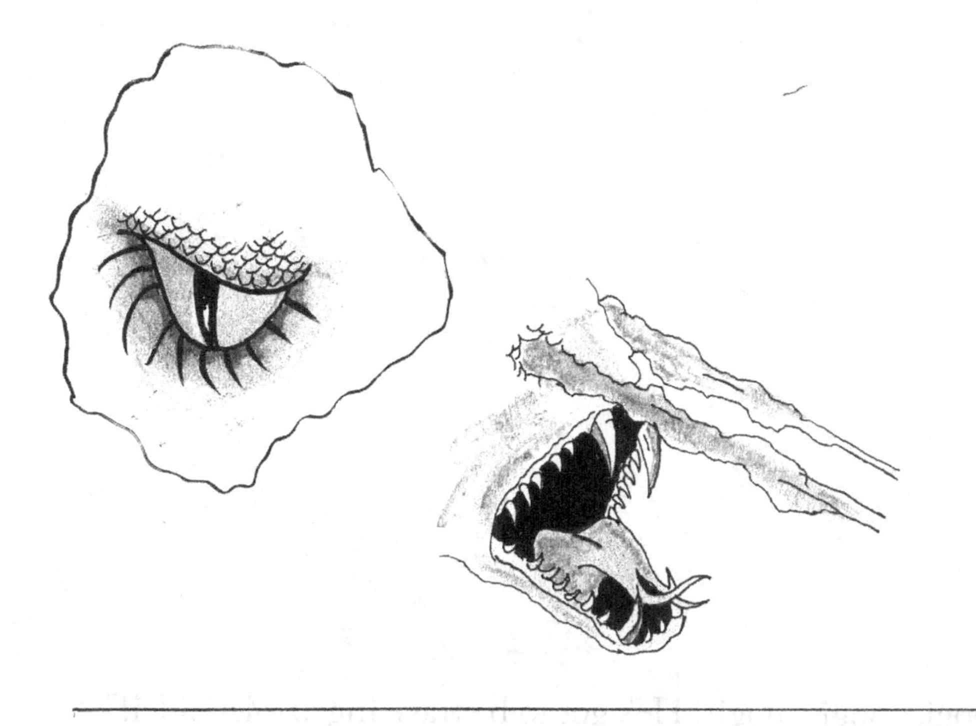

"Captain, bogie, bogie, bogie! He's got to be traveling at MACH 1!"

"Bank left, bank left! Get the Hell out of his way!"

Both pilots aim and shoot, but the Dragon deploys his protective shield, deflecting the bullets.

"What the...? Why aren't we connecting? The bullets are bouncing off some kind of shield!"

With a mighty swing of his lethal tail, and a burst of fire from his nostrils, the Dragon succeeds in knocking Captain Allen's plane out of the air.

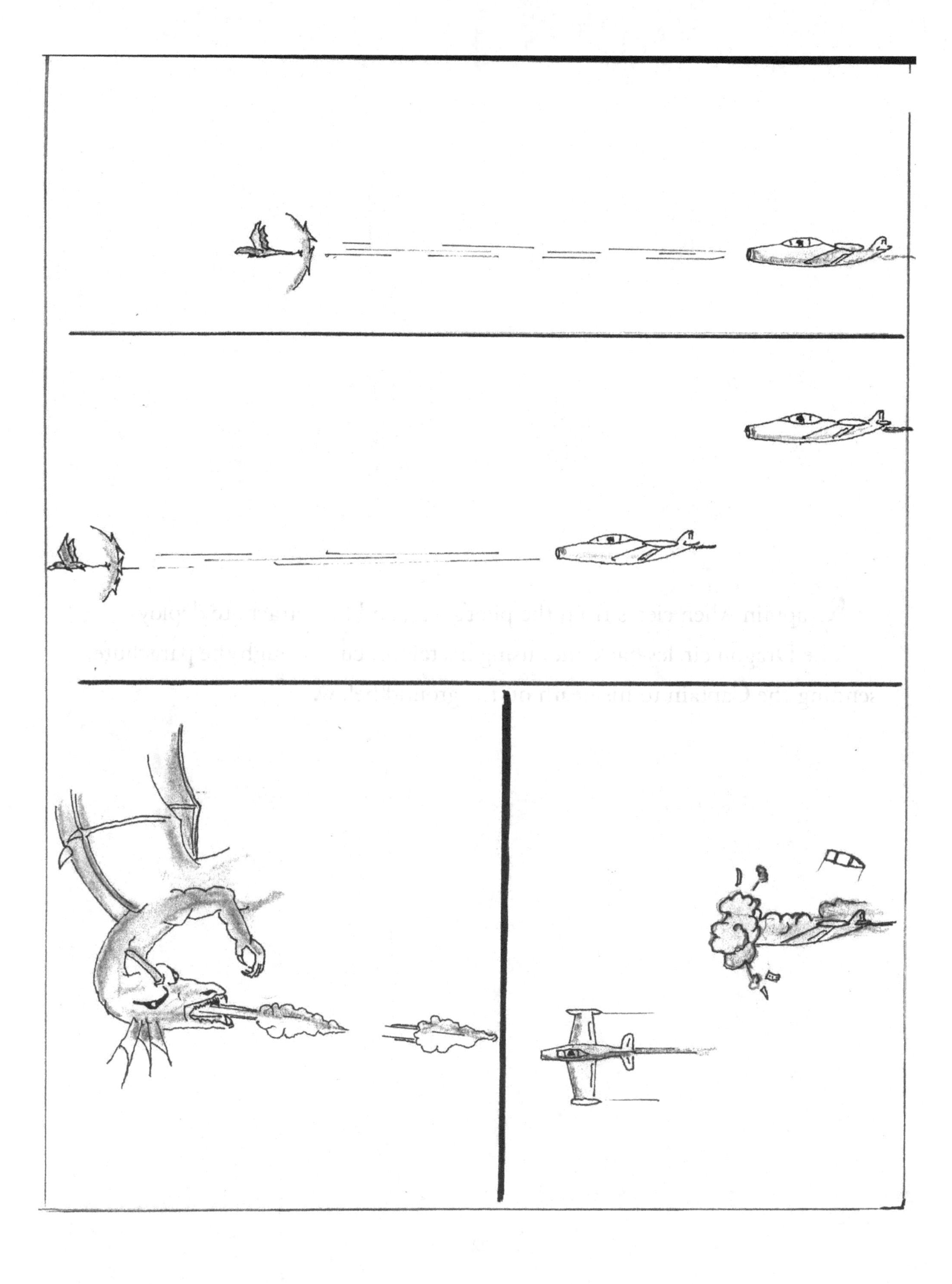

Captain Allen ejects from the pilot's seat, and his parachute deploys.

The Dragon circles back and, using his talons, cut through the parachute, sending the Captain to his death on the ground below.

AAAAAAA

Assembling the heads of state, a meeting is held to discuss how to deal with the Dragon.

"I'm not prepared to lose any more men!"

"How did we get into this mess in the first place? In this day and age...I mean, Christ, it's like a nightmare."

-We've tried everything we have. There's this protective damn shield that prevents anything from getting through..."

"It's going to take something new...a new weapon. Who can we go to? Isn't there somebody working on alternative weaponry?"

"What about those people in Nevada? Those UFO guys...don't they have something we haven't used... something lethal and secret?"

It was decided to take it to General Cal Dodds, a man who had experience with a wide variety of enemies.

"Yes, I absolutely agree. We have to pull out all the plugs, get the best men on this immediately. I happen to know that Captain Duffy and Sgt. Major Bills have been working with a group on air assisted bazooka-type weapons. Just prototypes up to now, but we've got to try whatever we've got."

Foot Trigger
COMPRESS AIR

And working quickly and quietly, Duffy and Bills moved ahead with their new weapon.

Where's Sergeant Major
Motor Poor Sir
Barracks 3
POOL

Work moved ahead at a rapid pace. The newest alloys and strongest metals were fitted together according to the secret plans.

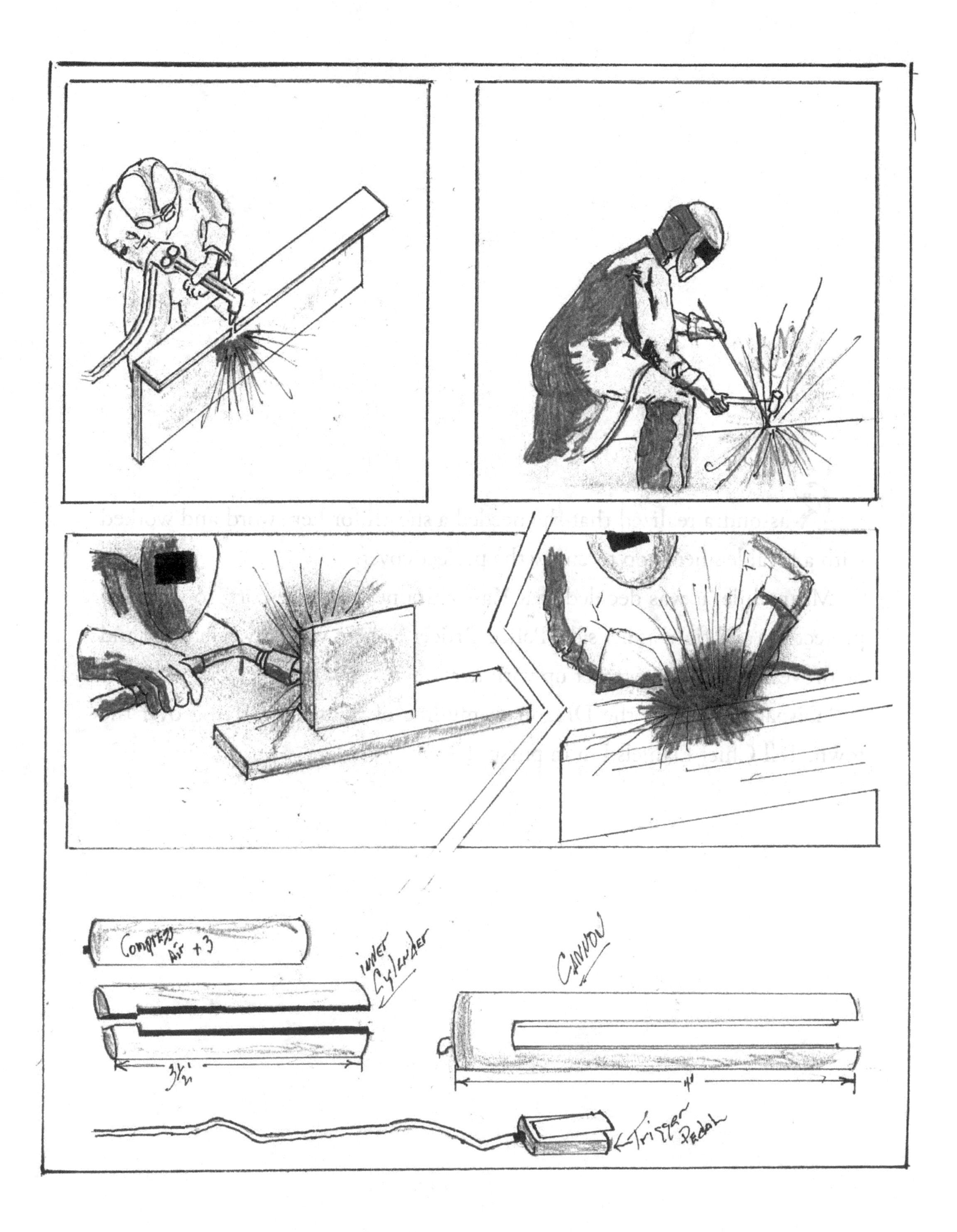
Compress Air +3
inner Cylinder
3½'
CANNON
4'
Trigger Pedal

Kassondra realized that she needed a sheath for her sword and worked with a local leather shop to create the perfect cover.

Meanwhile, it was decided that Kassondra needed an escort, someone to protect her and fight at her side. Police Officer Robert Weber was selected and he drove across town to meet up with her.

"Dispatch! I've got the Dragon in my line of sight! He's flying over the town. Tell Chief Daniels I'm in pursuit!"

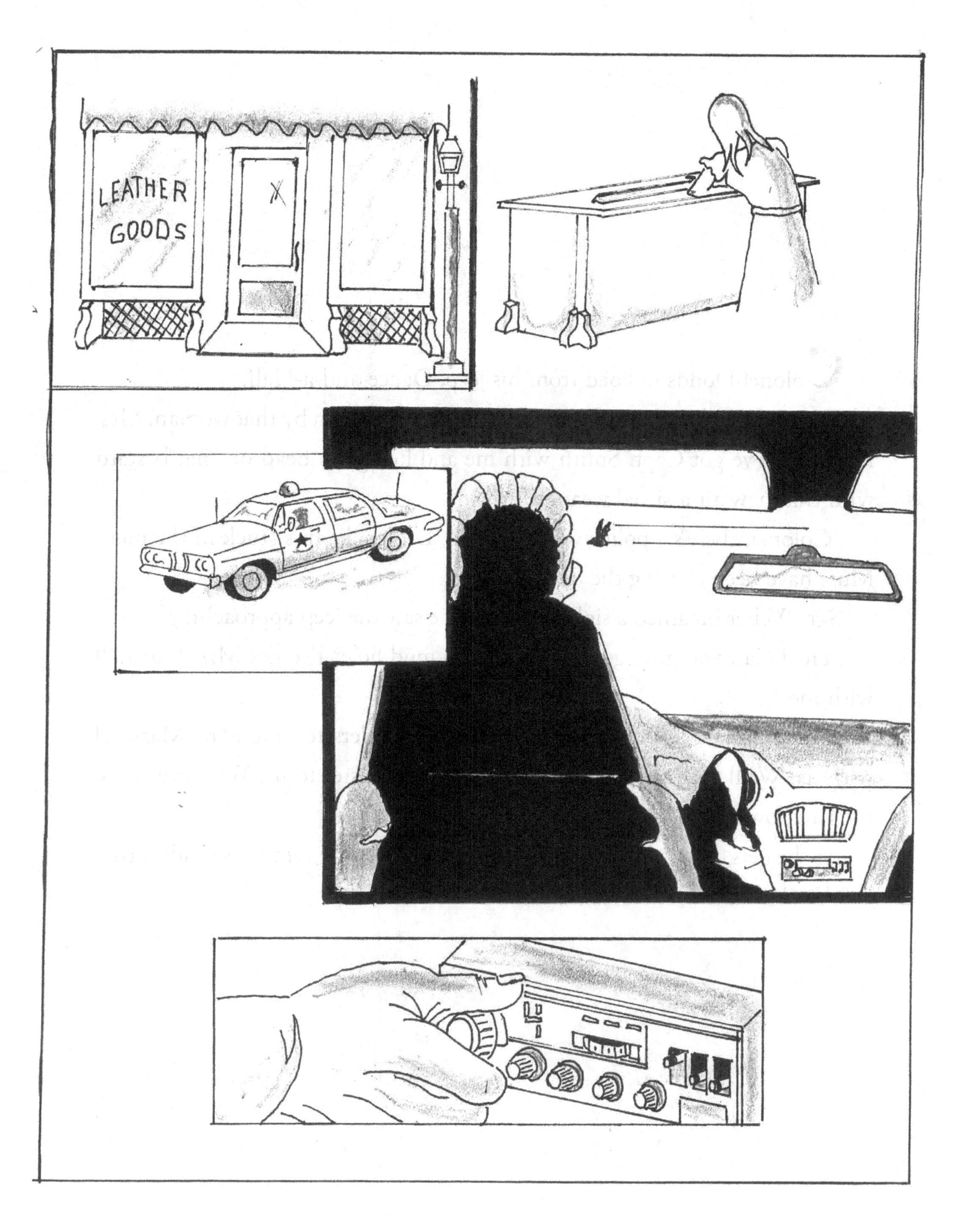
LEATHER
GOODS

Colonel Dodds radioed from his jeep, Deuce-and-a-Half.

"Keep all civilians out of the area. Don't let anyone in by that woman, Mrs. Marshall. I've got Capt. Smith with me and he's got a bead on that bastard with that new air assisted weapon."

"Colonel, there's a police vehicle ahead. Looks like he's stuck in the mud. Must have been chasing the dragon."

Sgt. Weber breathed a sigh of relief as he saw the jeep approaching.

"Hey! Can you guys get me out of this mud hole? I've got Mrs. Marshall with me."

"I'm Capt. Dodds from the base. We have orders to take Mrs. Marshall with us. We'll get you out, but you leave that monster to us. You haven't got the fire power."

As she gets out of the police case, Kassondra sees the Dragon's shadow pass overhead.

Soaring over the vehicles below, the Dragon spots Kassondra looking up at him.

"Ready to go again, lady?"

B Lit he was reluctant to make the first move because he remembered the shock he received from the sword.

He circled above, keeping his eyes on Kassondra.

The men in Deuce-and-a-Half looked up. Capt. Smith fine-tuned his aim.

Kassondra help up her arms and shouted at the Dragon.

"I don't have my sword! You've won. You've conquered our world. Why aren't you proud? Hold up your head and show us all how proud you are of your victory!"

The military men knew what she was trying to do. If the Dragon looked up...held his head high...they might be able to get a shot at his soft underbelly.

And the Dragon obliged. He raised his head high, preparing to sound his battle shriek...and they fired the new weapon!

AAAAAA

. . . In that instant, as the Dragon went down, the Time Portal opened—

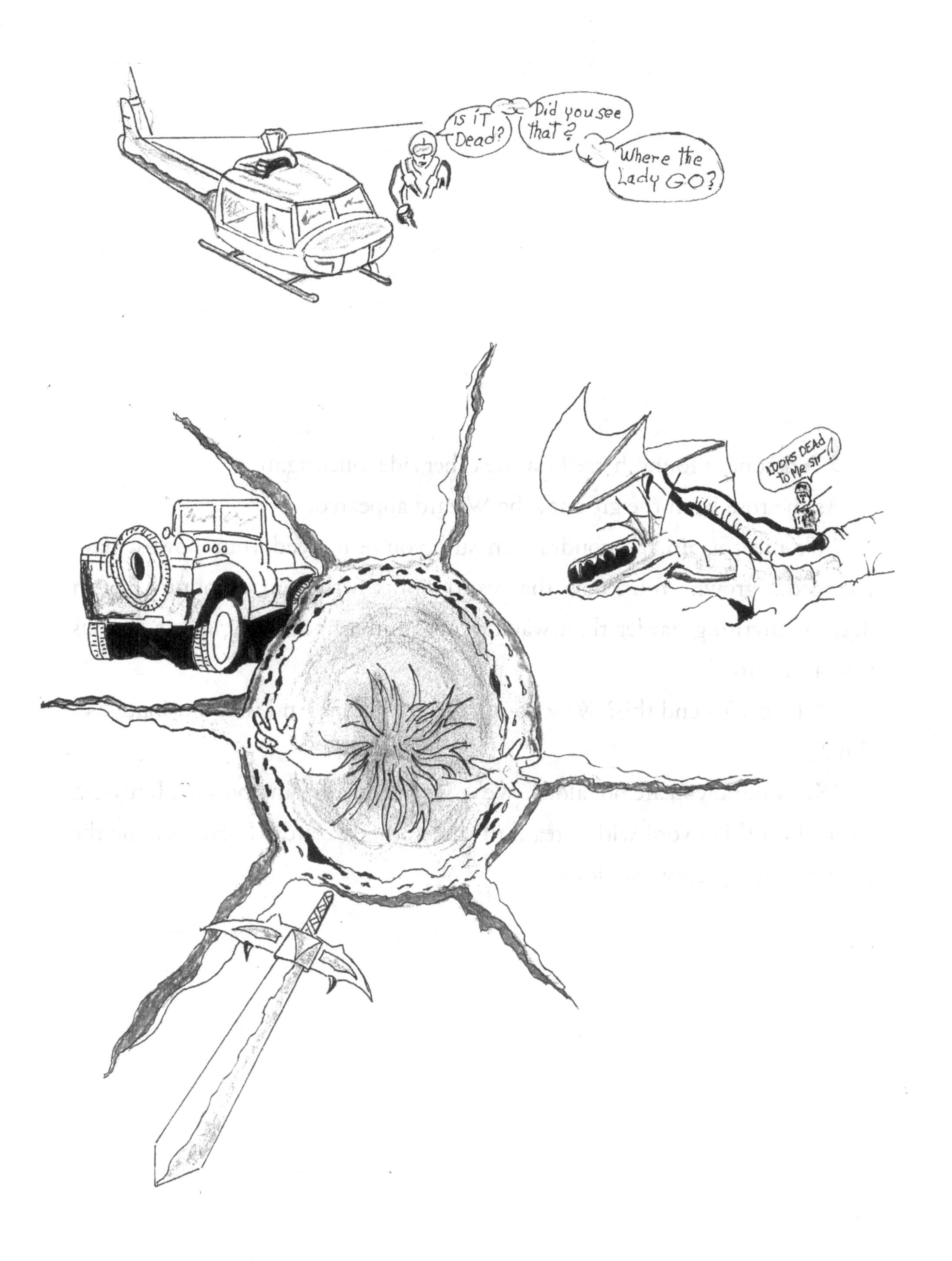
Is IT Dead?
Did you see that?
Where the Lady GO?
LOOKS DEAd To Me sir!!

Kassondra found herself on the other side, once again.

As she rose from the ground, the Wizard appeared.

"We meet again, Kassondra. I'm sure you've noticed your powers have changed... grown. You know the sword works with your emotions. It can destroy anything harder than water. And, more importantly, it can heal as well as destroy."

"Why can't I end this? Why does it go on and on? And why am I alone in this'?"

"Kassondra, you are not alone. We've given you amazing powers. I, myself, worked on this sword with a team of three other wizards. It can assume the power of any enemy you destroy."

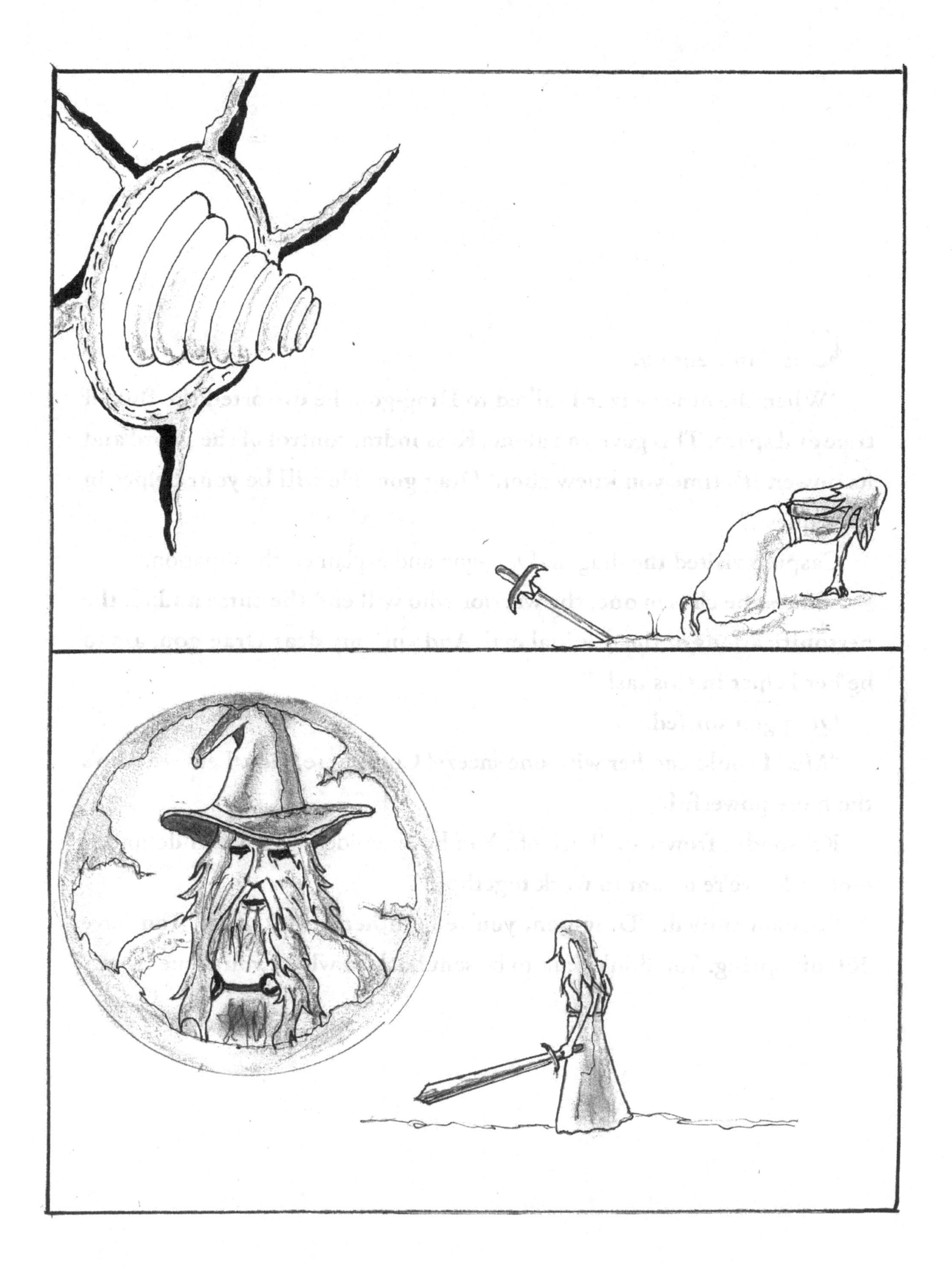

Caspian went on.

"When the other wizard talked to Drag-gon, he distorted the flux of time and space. This gave you alone, Kassondra, control of the sword and its power. It's time you knew about Drag-gon. He will be your helper in your quest."

Caspian visited the dragon, Drag-gon and explained the situation.

"She is the chosen one, the warrior who will end the curse and all the personifications of the original evil. And you, my dear Drag-gon, are to be her helper in this task."

Drag-gon sniffed.

"Me!? I could end her with one sneeze! Come here, lady. Let's see who's the more powerful."

Kassondra frowned. "Back off. You have no idea what I can do and it looks like we're meant to work together."

Caspian smiled. "Drag-gon, you've been here 1000 years. You have 300 off-spring. You don't want to be sent back to where you came from."

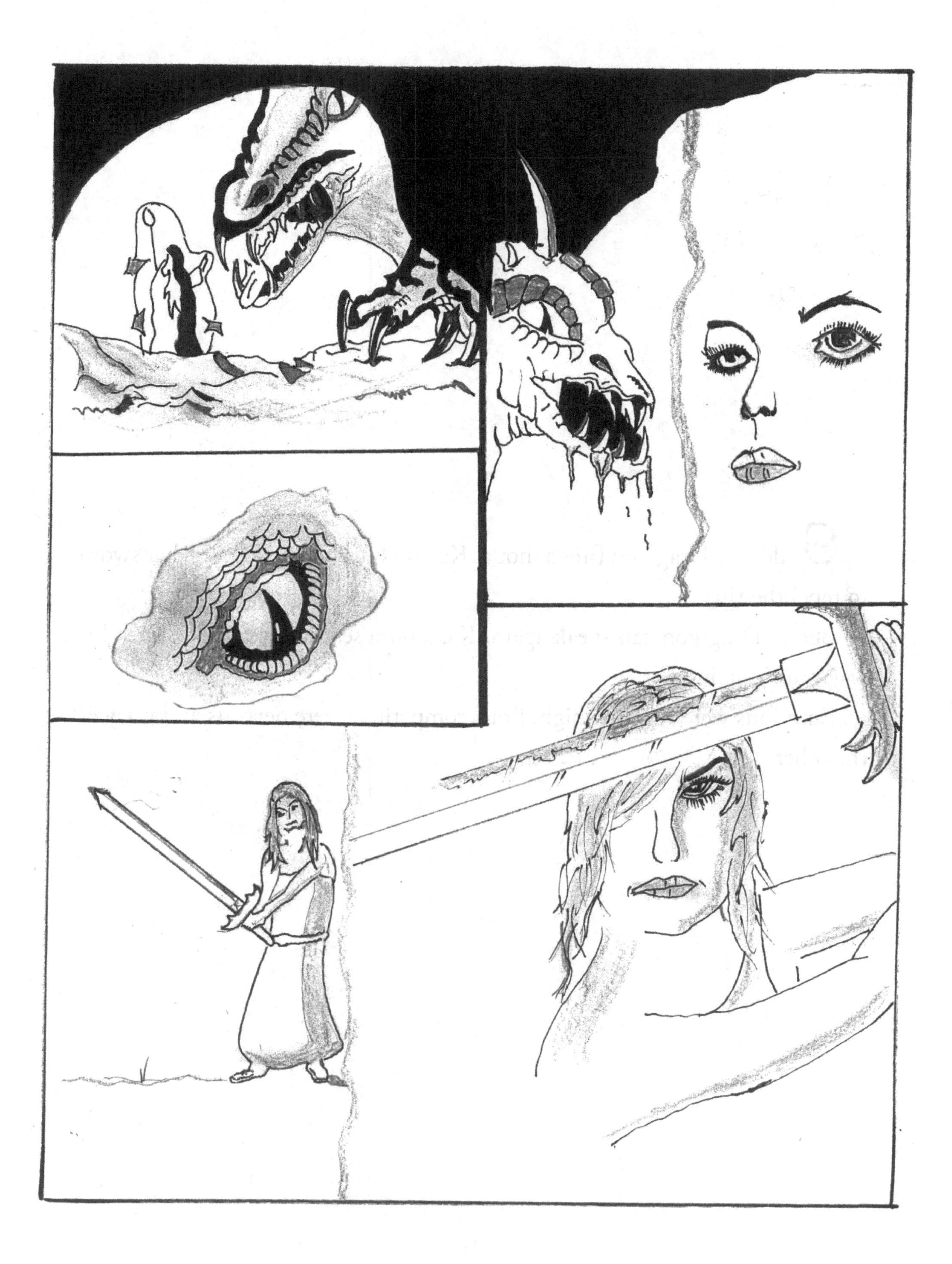

Suddenly Drag-gon fires a shot at Kassondra who quickly lifts her sword to repel the fire.

Before Drag-gon can speak again, Kassondra send an electrical shock his way, stunning him.

Emotions were running high. Both competitors were nervous and wary of the other.

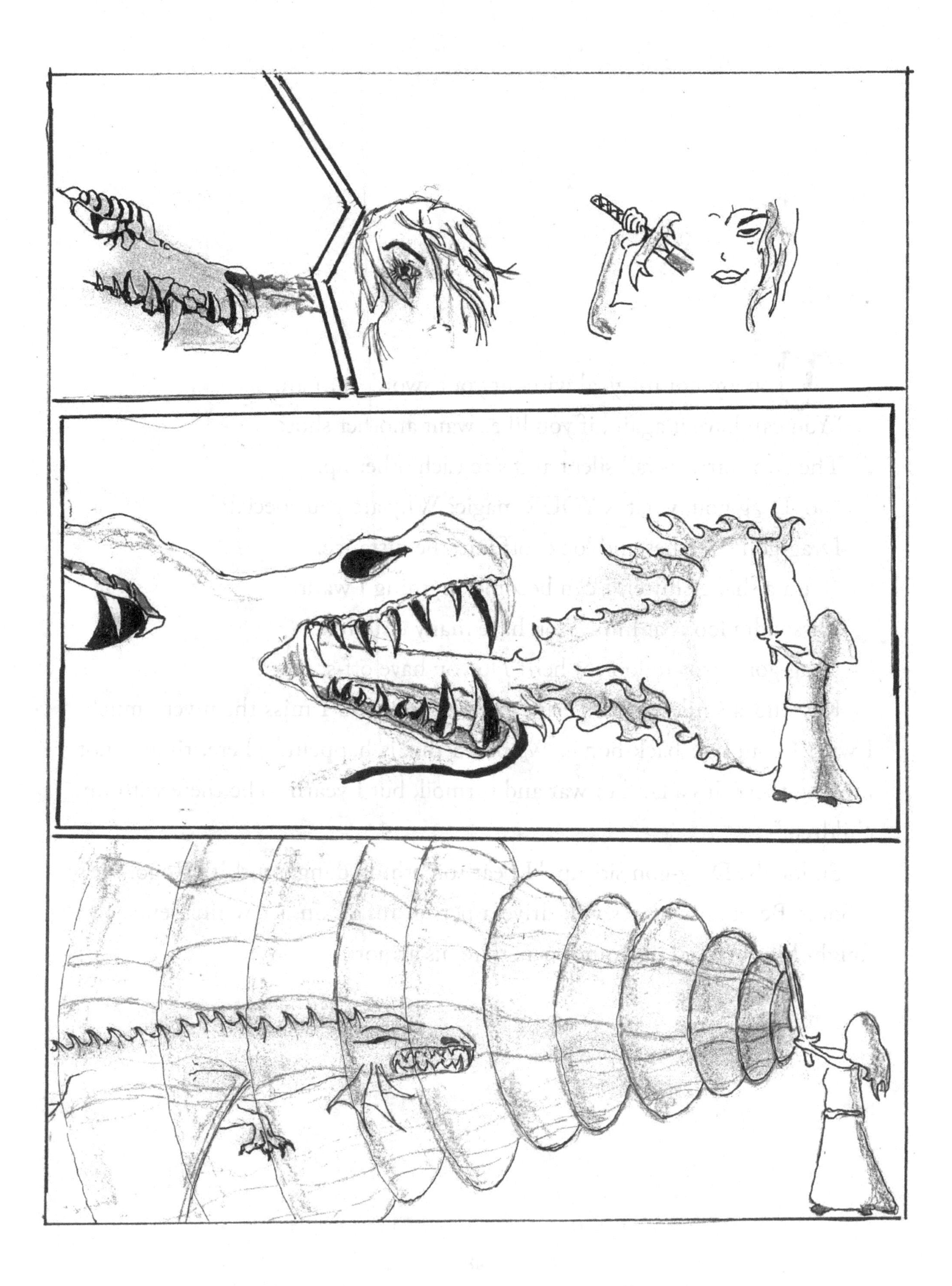

"You are not magical without your sword, human."

"You can have it again, if you like...want another shot?"

The two warriors fall silent and size each other up.

"So, Drag-gon, what is YOUR magic? Why are you special?"

Drag-gon stretches and looks off into the distance.

"I am a shape-shifter. I can become anything I want."

Kassondra looks at him. "You have many children."

Drag-gon turns to look at her. "Do you have off-spring?"

Kassondra smiles. "Yes, I have two children and I miss them very much. I wish I could go back home. While all this is happening here, time is not moving there. It's a land of war and turmoil, but I yearn to be there with my children."

Suddenly, Drag-gon sits up. "I hear something dangerous! It's Rogo! He's a Sonic Beast...his noises will drive a person insane in a few moments. I've fought him before but cannot penetrate his armor!"

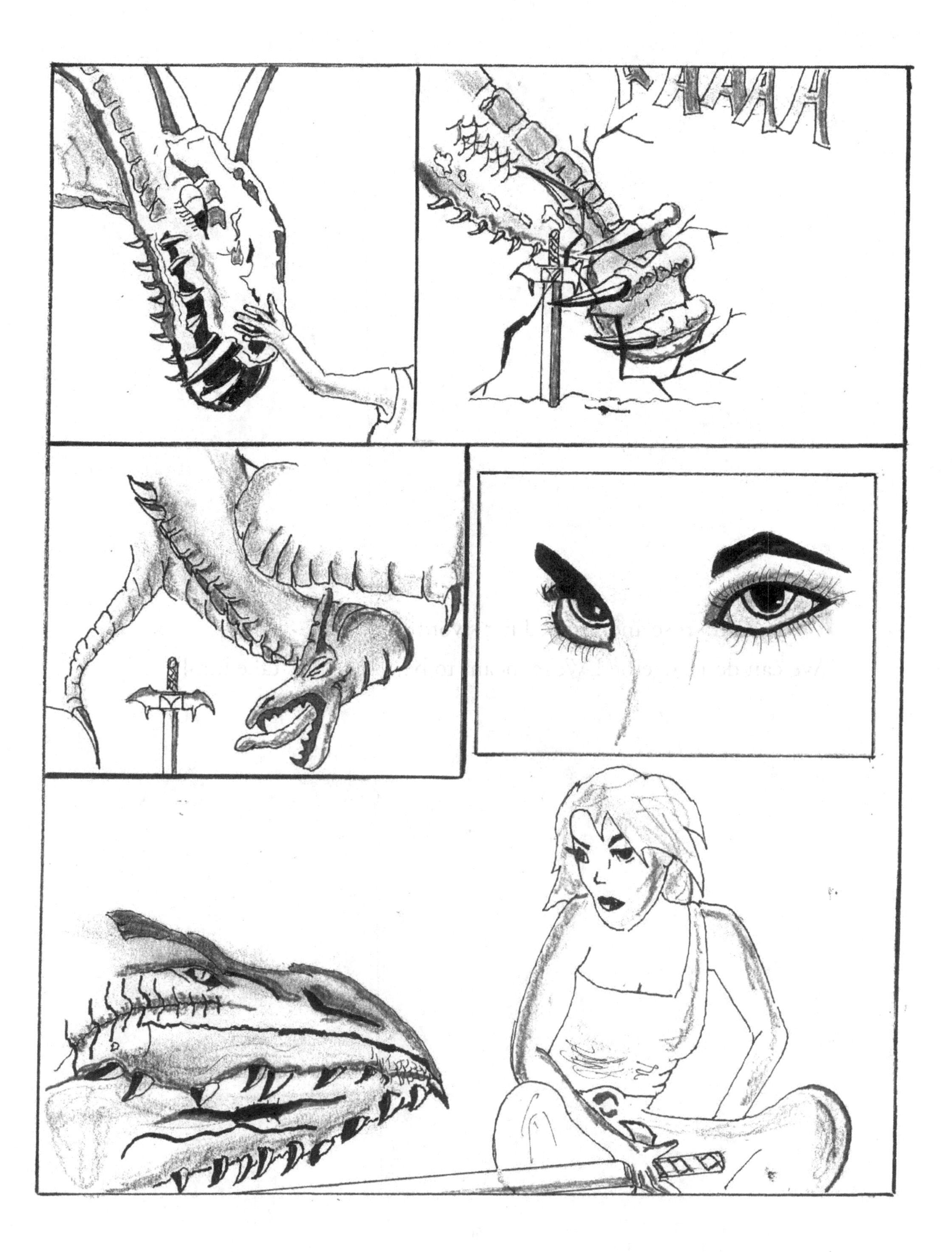
AAAA

Kassondra rose and gripped her sword.

"We can do it together! We're meant to be allies. Let's take him!"

As if communicating telepathically, the two position themselves strategically. Above them, hundreds of dragons begin to hatch and fly about.

Drag-gon and Kassondra let go with everything they've got.

Kassondra sent shock wave after shock wave of electricity into Rogo and Drag-gon enveloped him in fire.

Rogo is destroyed!

Drag-gon smiles at the sky full of little dragons.

"Rogo kept food and water from other dragons. Survival was very tenuous. Now he is dead and we can live free again. Thank you for your help, Kassondra."

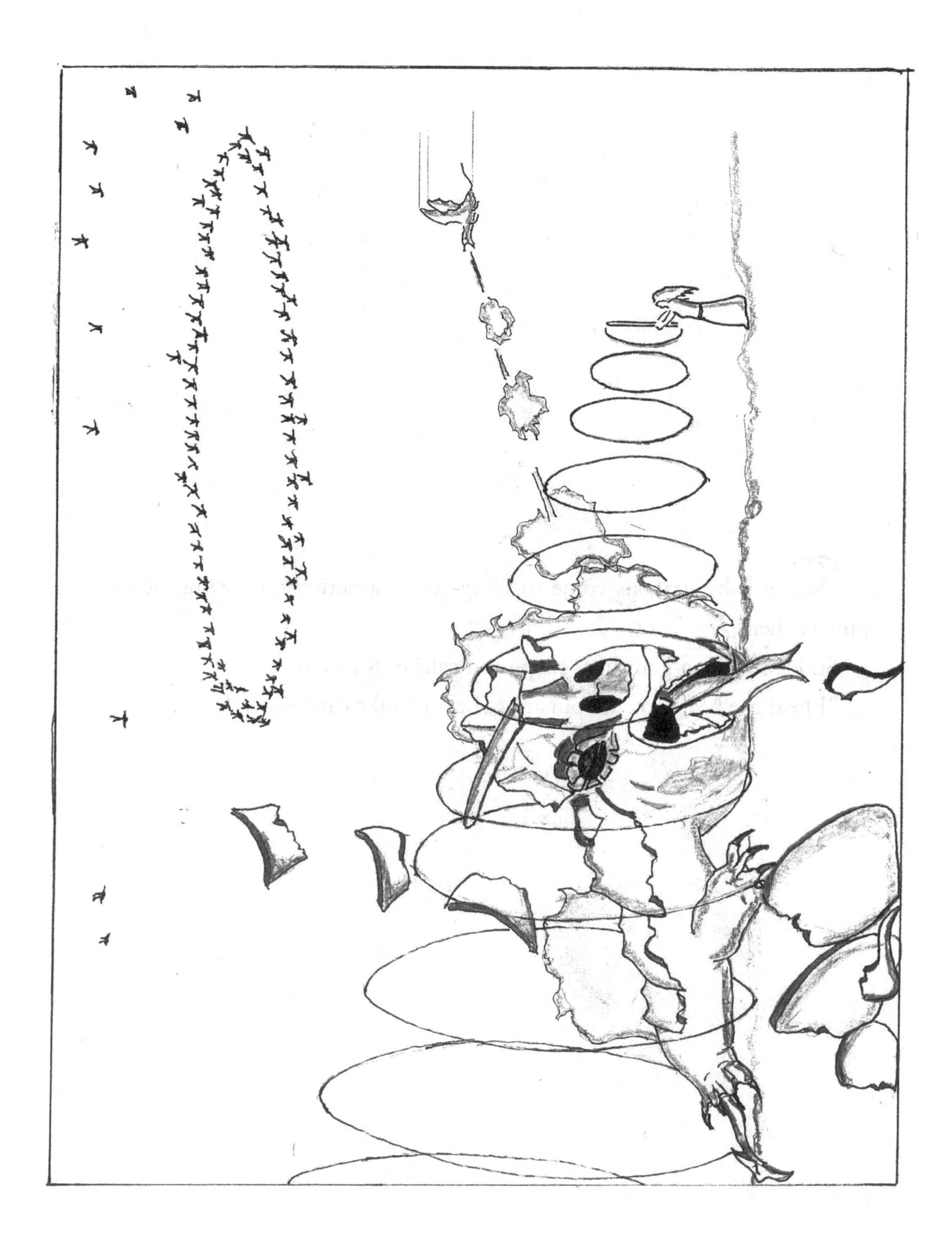

The baby dragons come to Drag-gon instinctively, knowing he will protect them.

Suddenly, Drag-gon shifts shape and calls to Kassondra.

"I hear the beast you are pursuing! Let's go take care of her!"

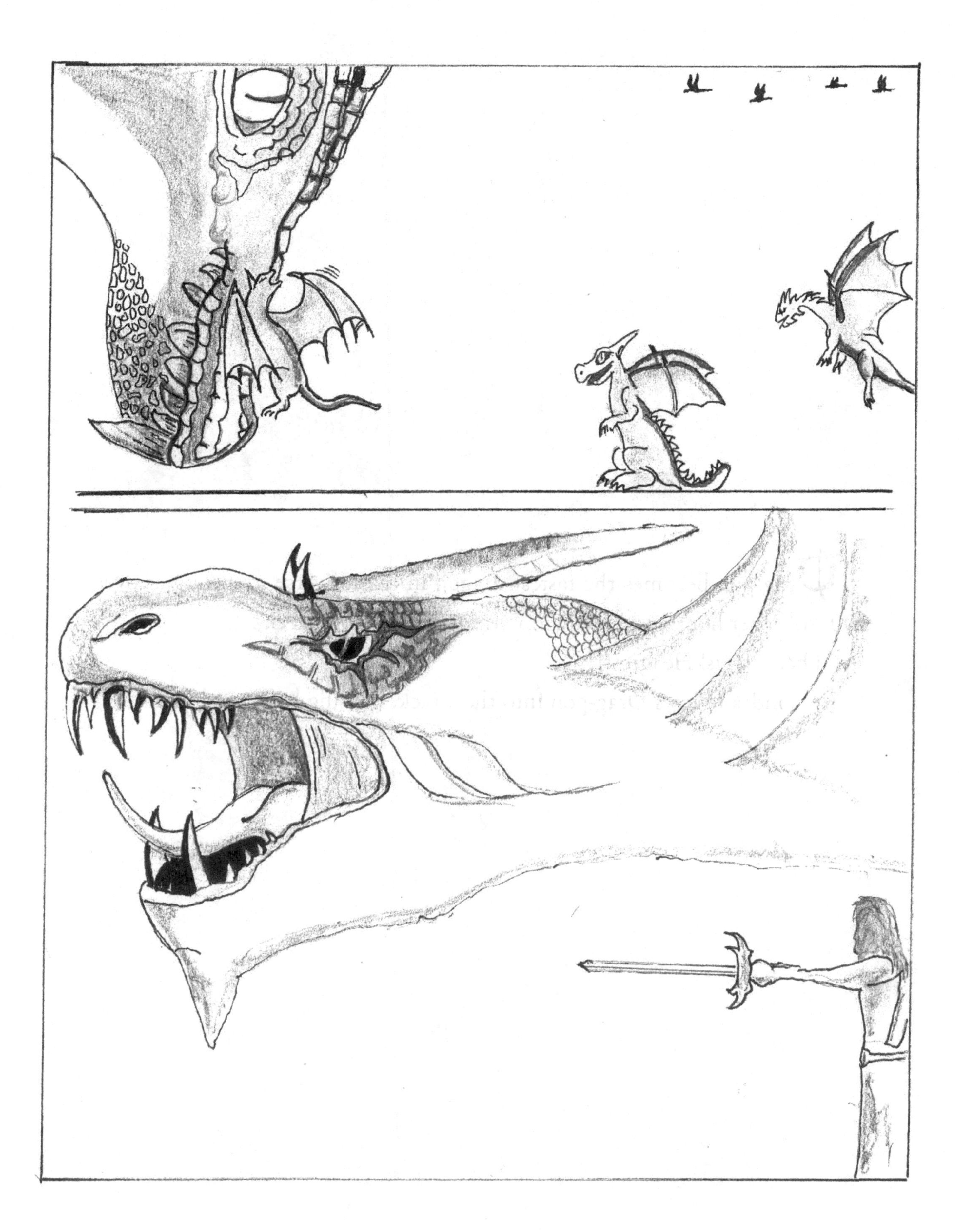

Drag-gon becomes the fastest dragon in the universe, traveling at over 200 miles per hour and his dragon armor morphs into steel.

"There she is! Heagress!"

Kassondra follows Drag-gon into the attack, holding her sword high.

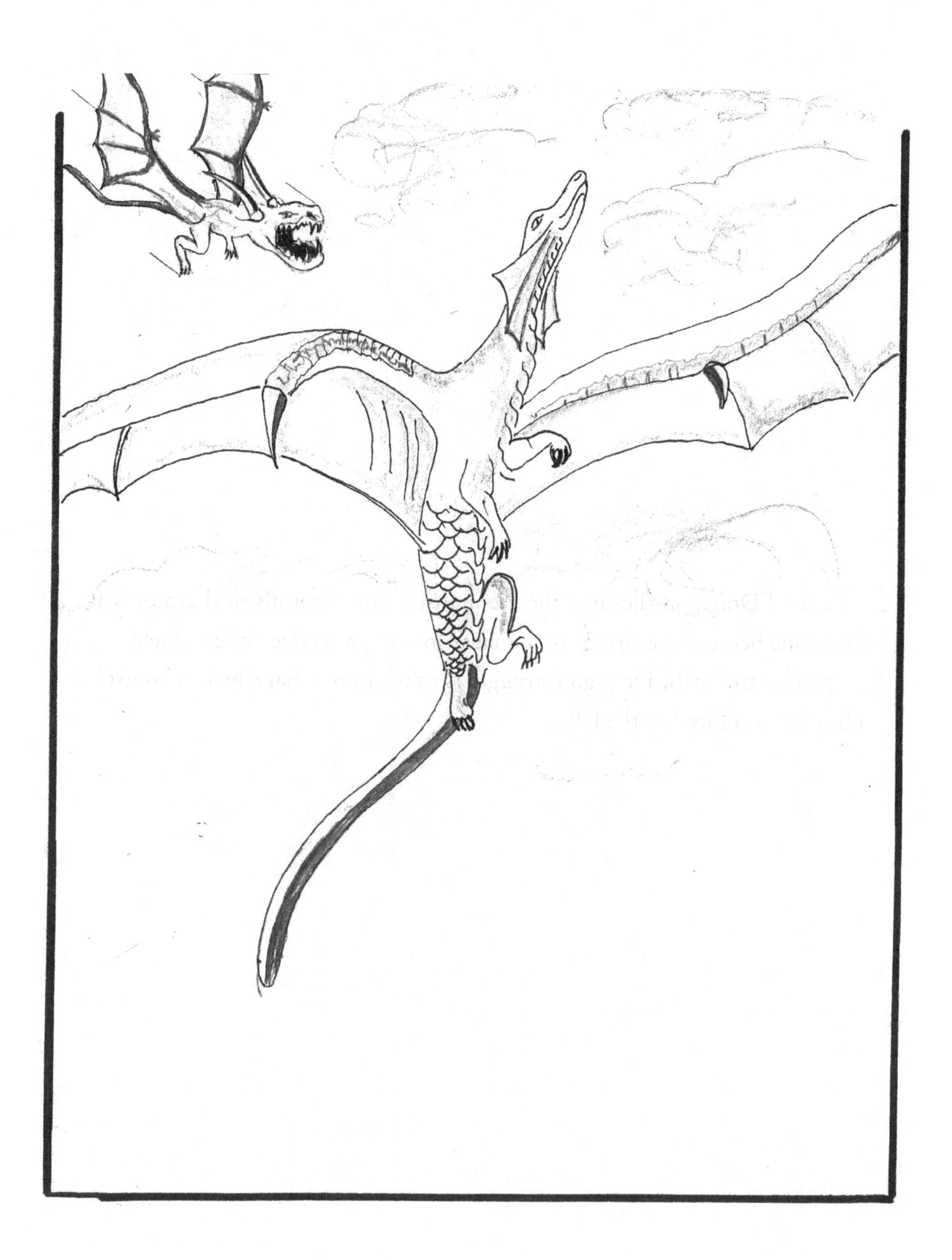

And Drag-gon flies into the she-monster, confident his steel armor will overcome her. But the armor is no match for her protective bubble shield.

Falling to Earth, Drag-gon struggles to shift into a shape he can control. His neck is injured in the fall.

Kassondra rushes to his side.

"You're injured! Let me help you."

Kassondra remembers that her sword now has healing power.

"No, no, your sword hurts me! Just give me some time to heal."

Kassondra examines his neck. "It's worse than you think it is. I must try my healing powers. Please."

Drag-gon agrees and his neck is healed by Kassondra's sword.

Drag-gon is grateful and tries his powers of flight.

He takes off in a powerful up-draft. Kassondra smiles and waves at him overhead.

From the skies, Drag-gon hears the cries of a baby dragon.

Ten Days Later

Suddenly, Heagress is back! Seeing her, knowing about her cruelty, Drag-gon instinctively wants to fight!

He engages her in a brief fire-fight.

As they circle each other, something magical about the female begins to change Drag-gon.

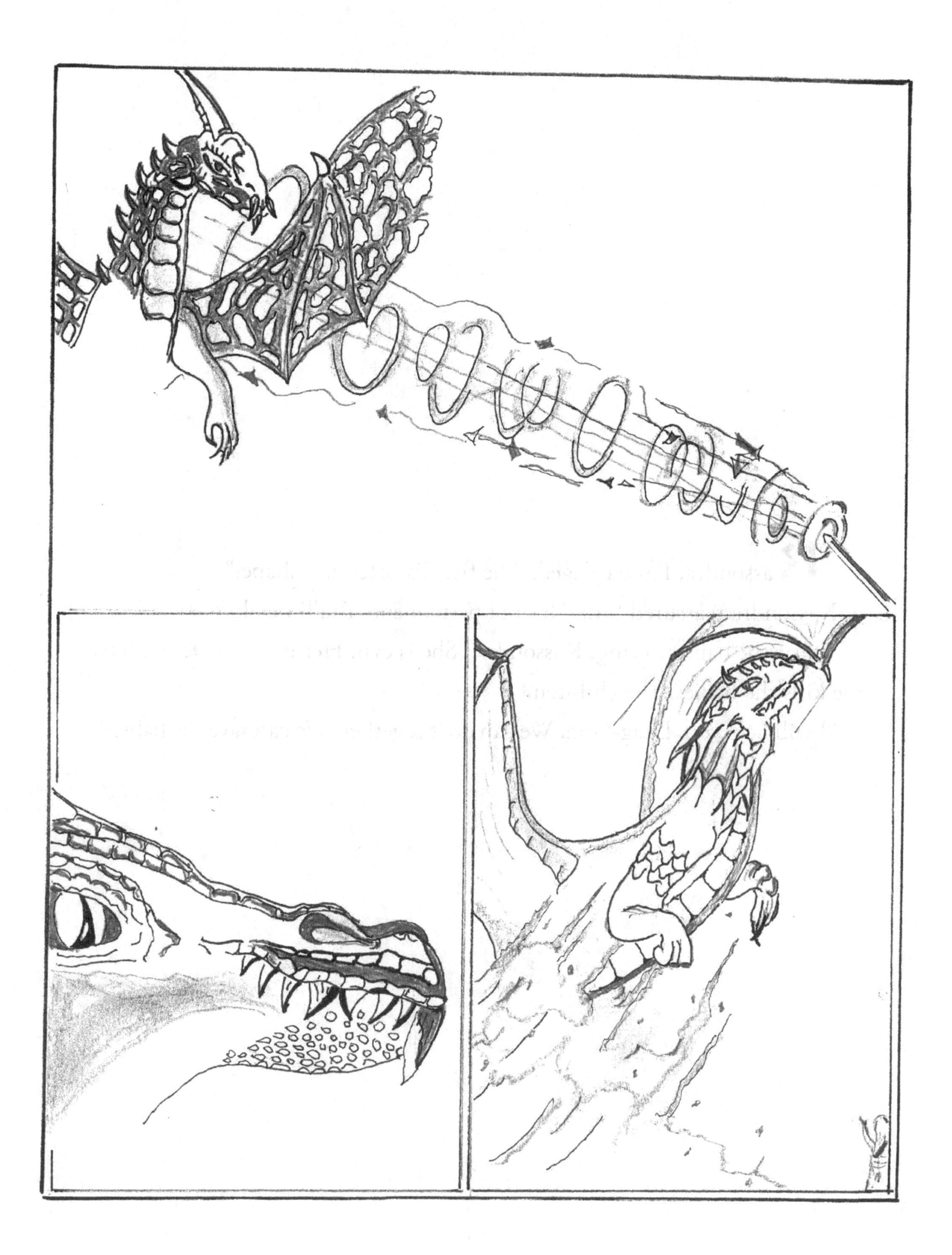

"Kassondra, I'm damaged. The fire distorted my shape!"

Kassondra reassured him. "It's not permanent. You'll be ok."

"Hear the babies crying, Kassondra?! She is evil. Her name is Demonicus. She kills the babies...the children.

"I will help you, Drag-Gon. We can do it together. We can save the babies!"

Drag-Gon frowns. "I've changed, Kassondra. It's changed me some way. Look at me...my shape changes with my mood! I'm vulnerable, weak!"

"No, no. You can make this work for you! As long as you live a good life, have good, caring feelings—as you do now—you'll be soft and vulnerable. But when you fight, when you feel those feelings, you'll be as powerful as you ever were! Think about all the pain Demonicus has caused...all the babies who have suffered under her!"

And Drag-Gon let himself feel the hatred and disgust he held for Demonicus. Changing into a mighty fighting dragon, he and Kassondra let loose all their power on Demonicus.

And she was destroyed.

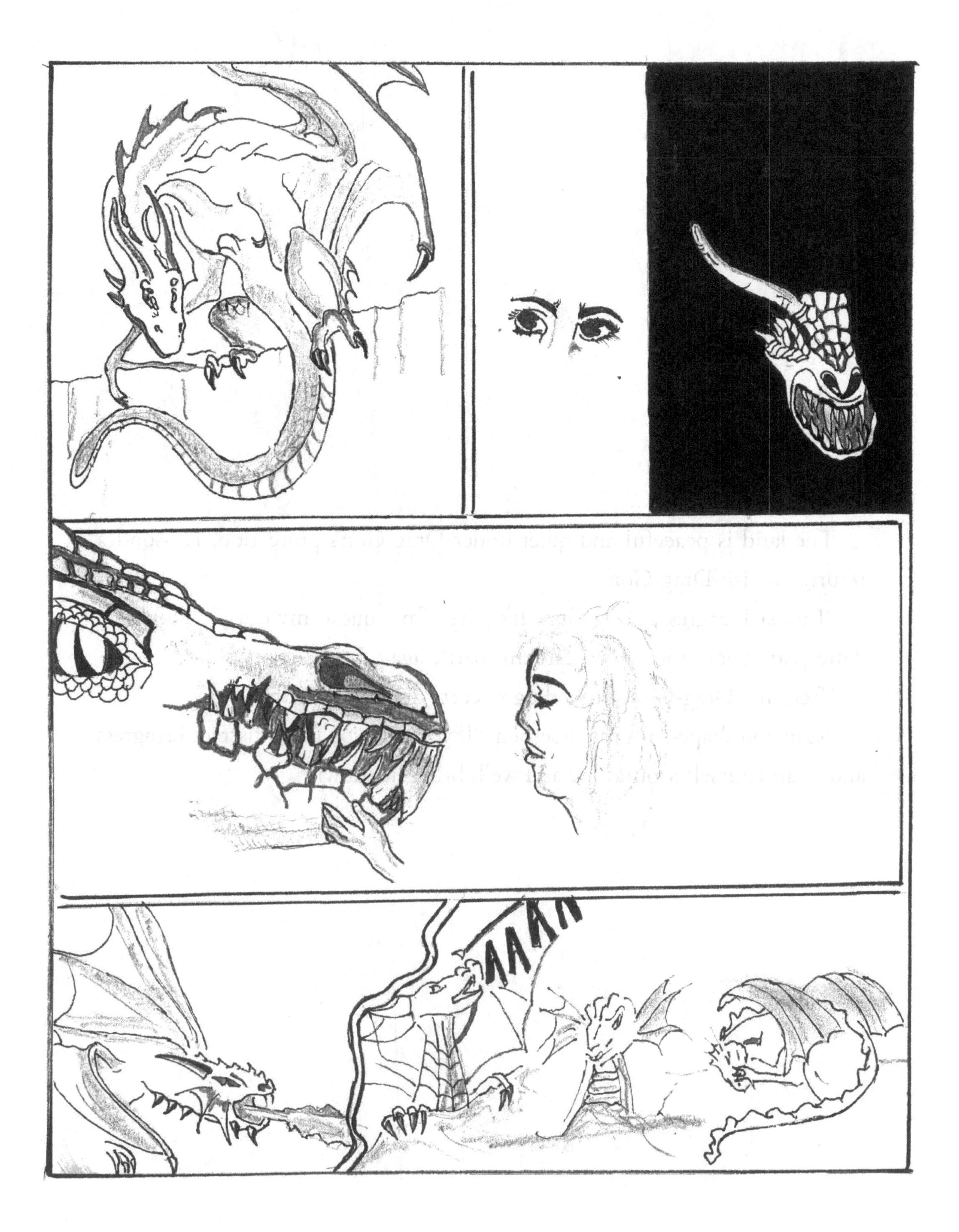
AAAA

Seven years later...

The land is peaceful and quiet under Drag-Gon's protection. Kassondra returns to visit Drag-Gon.

"I must Heagress, Drag-Gon. It's part of my quest, my duty." "Don't go. Things are good now, don't start this battle again."

"Tell me, Drag-Gon, can a dragon carry another dragon? "No."

"Can you shape-shift into a serpent? If you can, you must distract Heagress and wrap yourself around her and we'll bring her down."

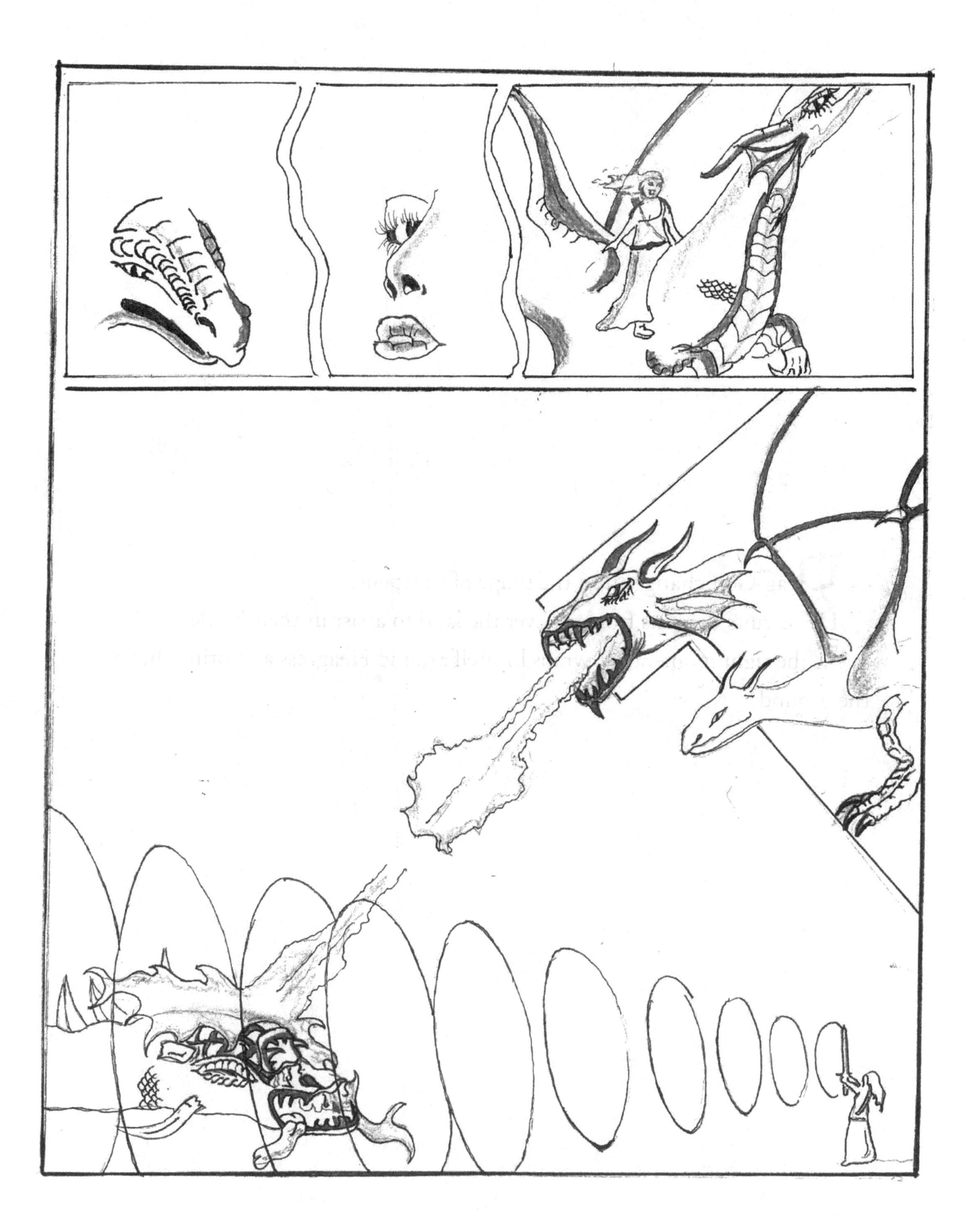

Drag-Gon changes into the shape of a serpent.

He recruits dragons from all over the land to assist in their battle.

At the right moment, he wraps himself around Heagress and brings her to the ground.

7 Year's Later

As they hit the ground together, both are seriously injured by the impact.

BA
BA
BA
BA
BA
BA

Kassondra asks the other dragons to help prop Drag-Gon up so she can heal him with her sword.

All the dragons are happy that Drag-Gon is still alive. He has been their protector...like a father to them all.

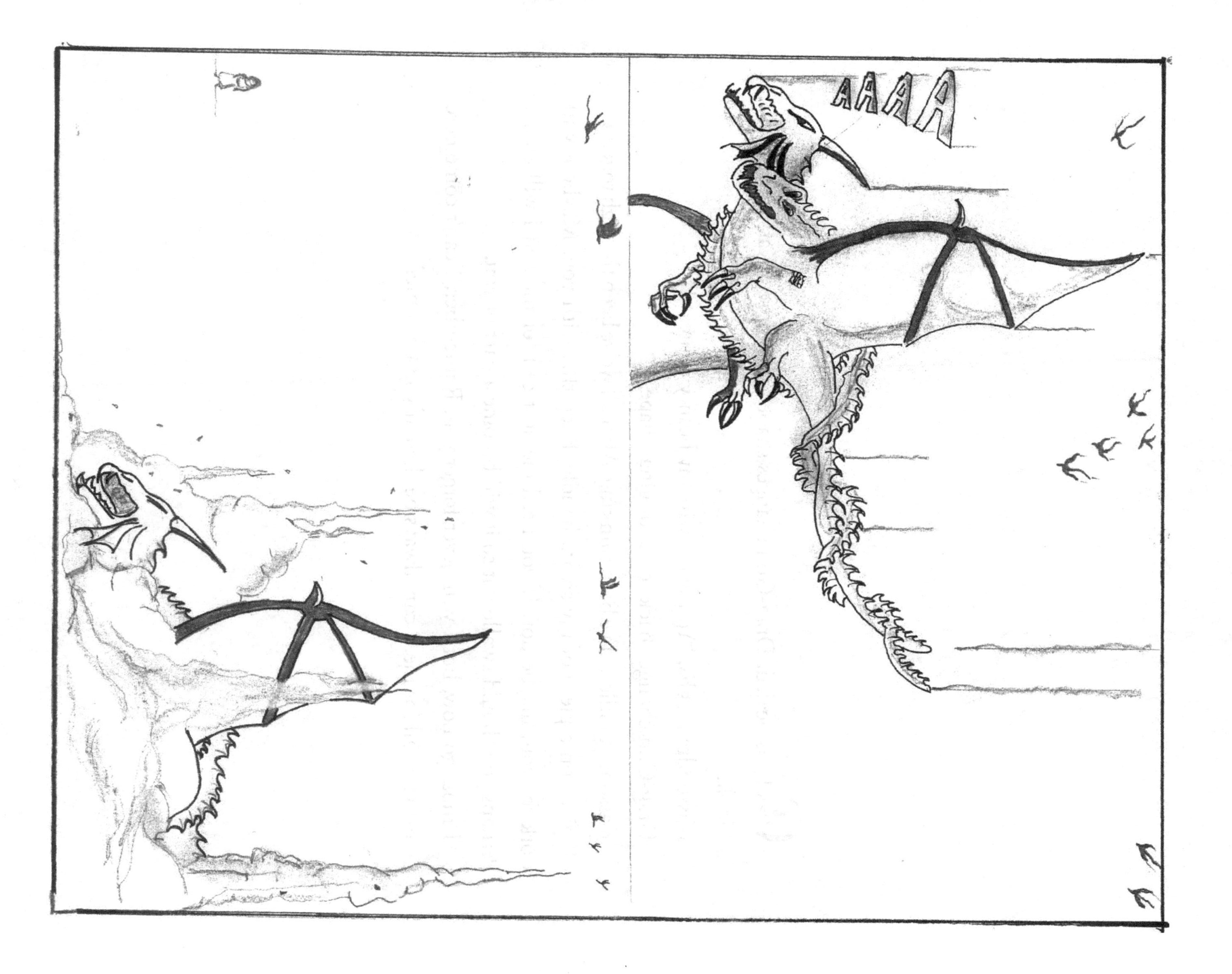
AAAA

As he is healed, Drag-Gon changes shape once more. “Kassondra, how do I look?’

Kassondra laughs. “You won’t win any beauty contests!”

Drag-Gon changes back to his original shape.

Kassondra smiles. “I’ve been thinking. After all we’ve been through together, I’ll give you a piece of my sword handle. Keep this with you. Maybe it will work for you, maybe not. If you need me, just call for me and I will come. Perhaps you should swallow it so it will become a part of you.

I must go now, but I will never forget you. Remember, I can’t come here unless you call for me. I can always be there if you need me.”

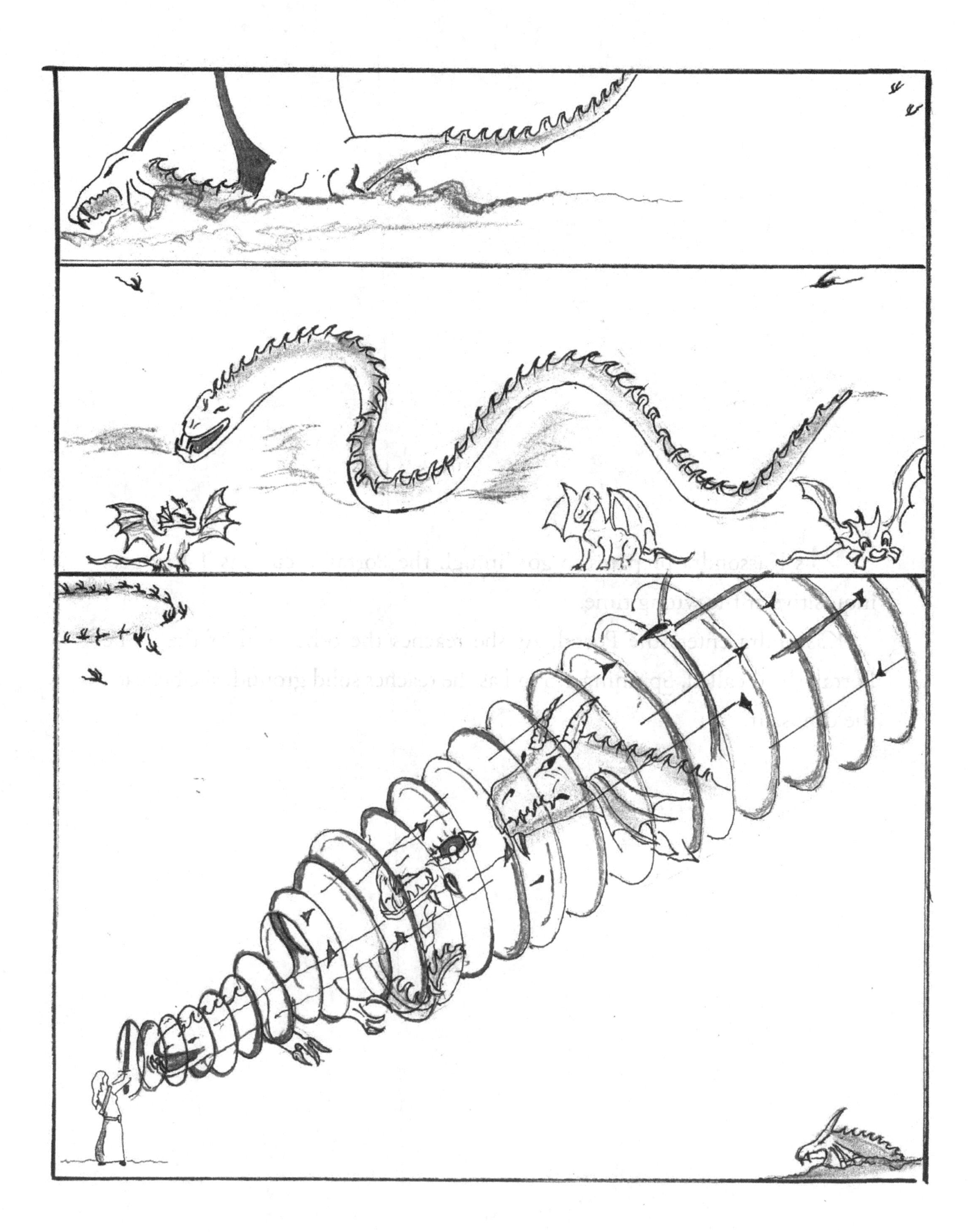

As Kassondra prepares to go through the Portal, a curious T-Rex gets inquisitive at the wrong time.

Kassondra enters the Portal. As she reaches the other end of the Time Portal, she is called. Spinning around as she reaches solid ground, she beheads the dinosaur.

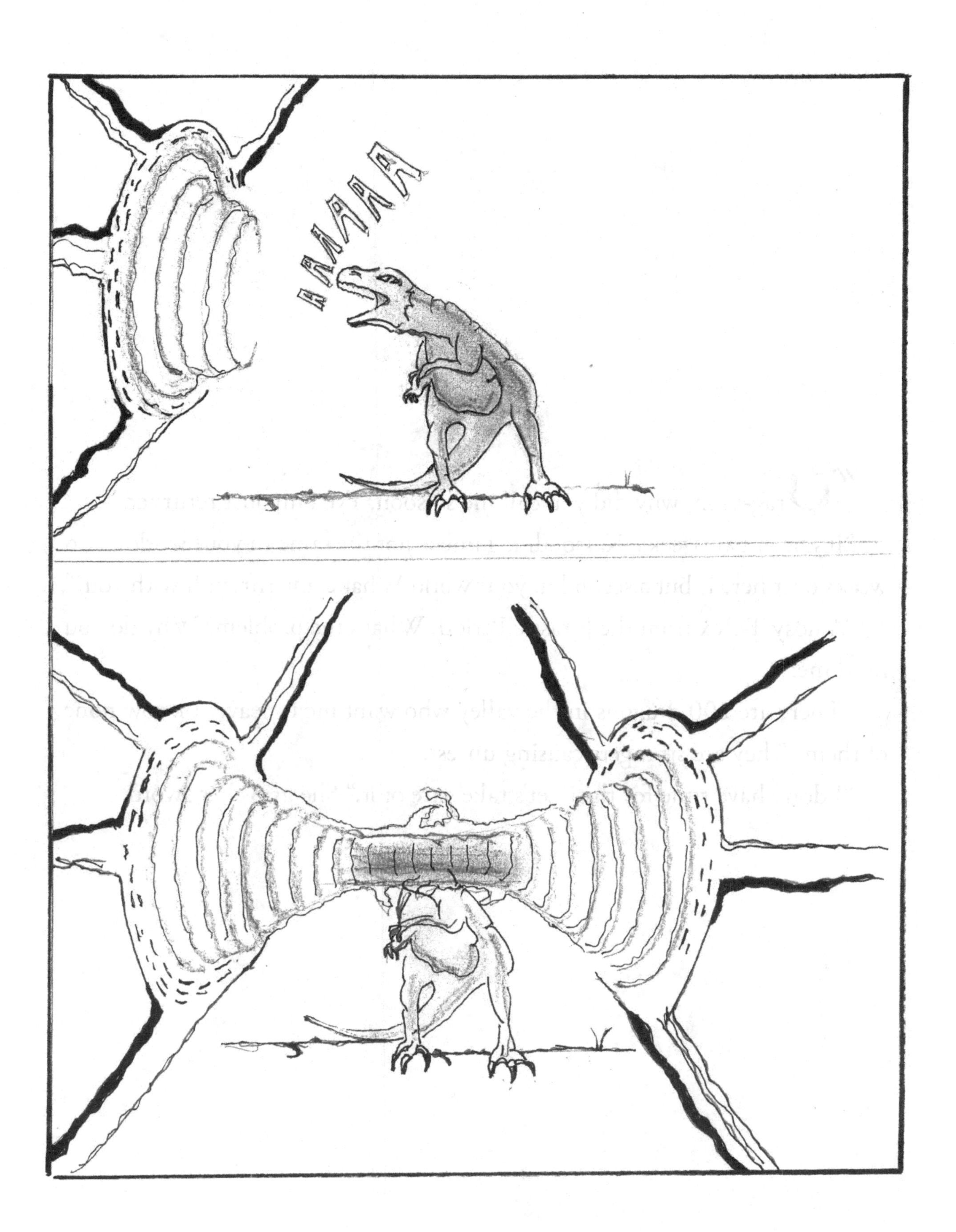

"Drag-Gon, why did you call me so soon? I've only just returned."

"It's been two weeks, Kassondra. Time is not the same in your world. Two weeks over here is but a second in your world What came through with you?"

"A nosy T-Rex from the Jurassic Period. What's the problem? Why do you need me?"

"There are 200 dragons in the valley who want me to leave. I know none of them. They are strangers causing unrest."

"I don't have time for this! Let's take care of it." She grips her sword.

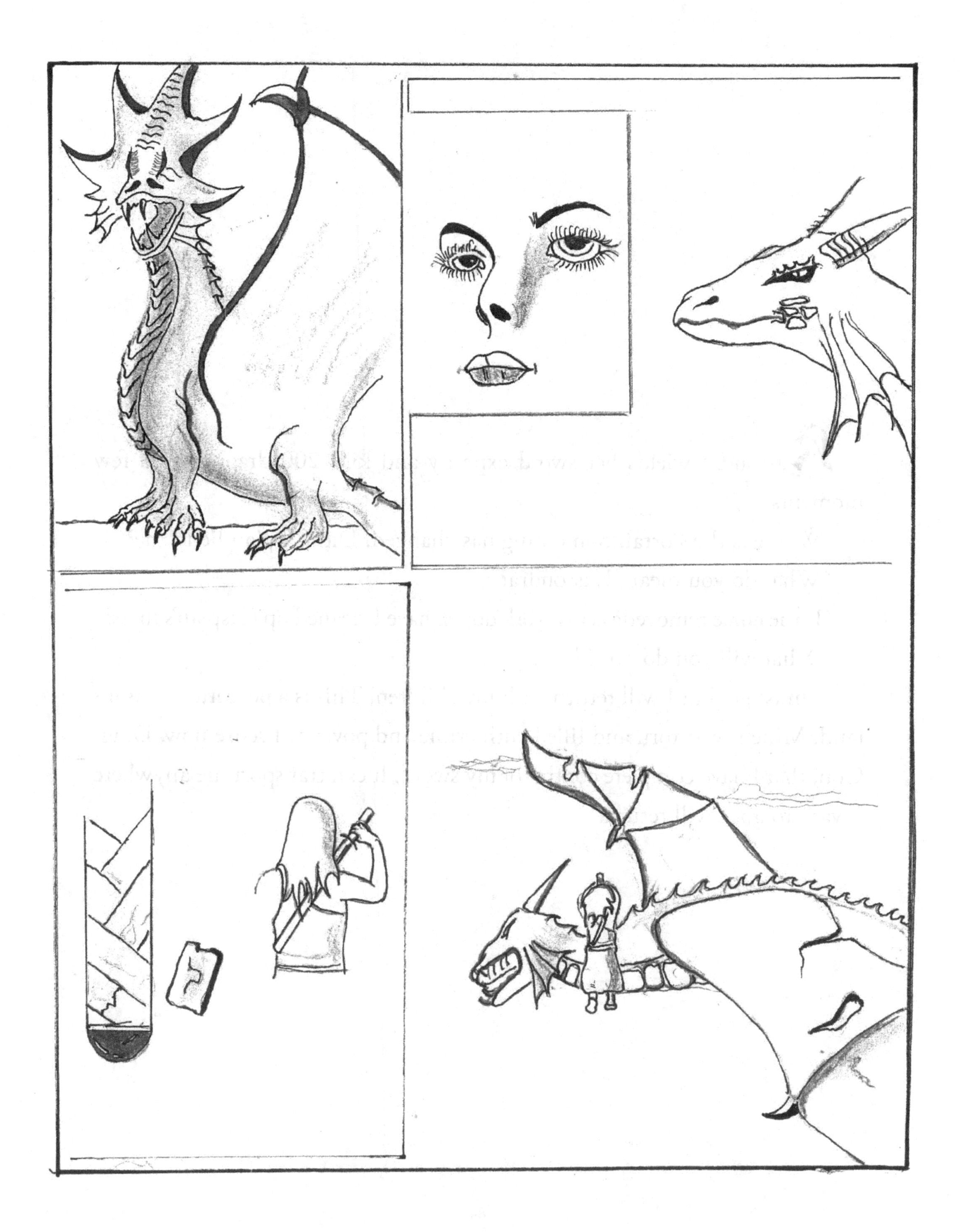

Kassondra wields her sword expertly and kills 200 dragons in a few moments.

"Where is the Portal? Something has changed. Did Caspian lie to me?

"What do you mean, Kassondra?"

"Is the curse removed? Is my work done...have I cleaned up Caspian's mess?"

"What will you do now?"

"I must go, but I will return with my children. This is a peaceful, pleasant land. Mine is war-torn and filled with crime and poverty. I sense now, Drag-Gon, that I have complete control of my sword. It can transport me anywhere I want to go. I will return."

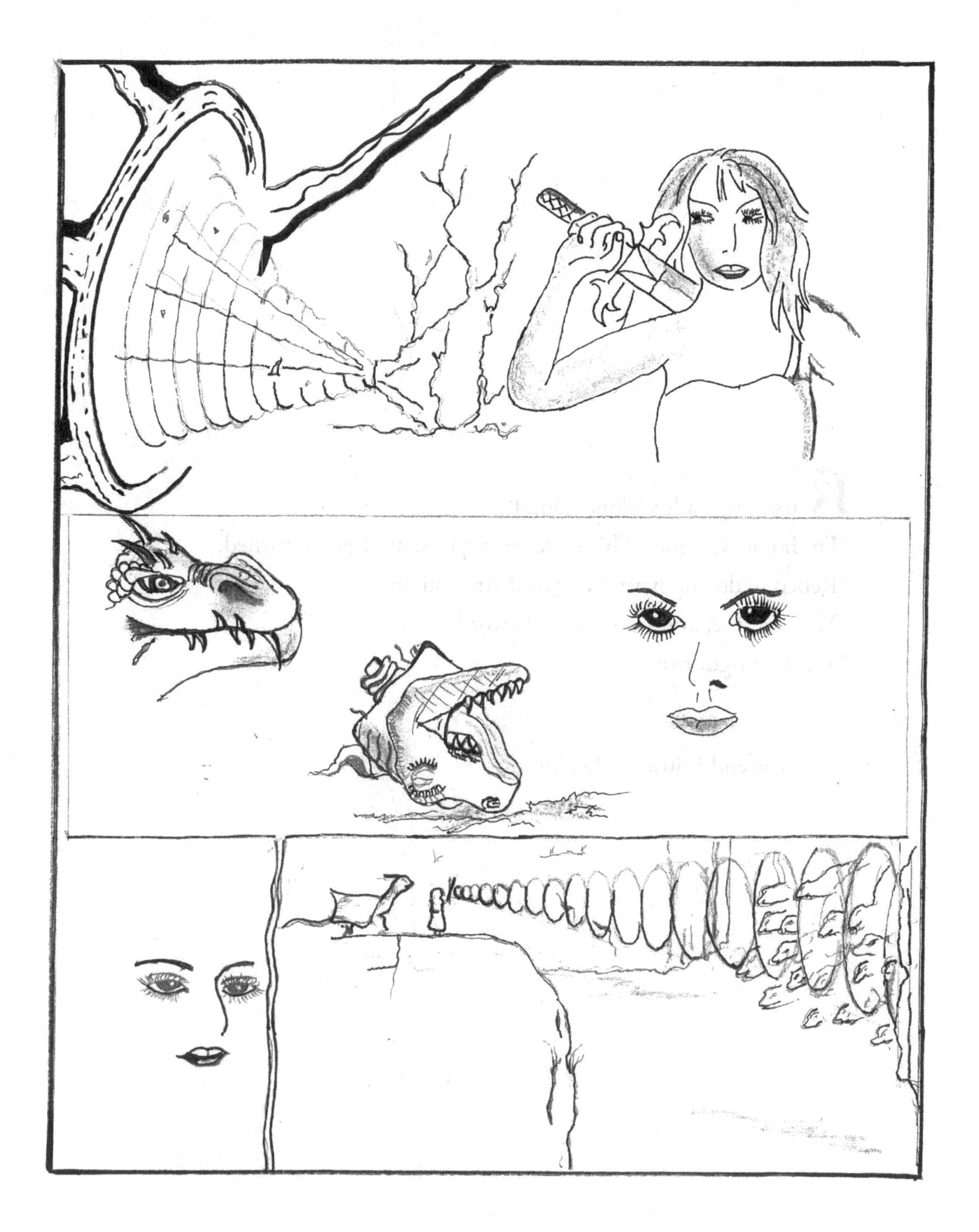

Kassondra calls Colonel Dodds.
"I'm home, Colonel. This is Rebecca Marshall. I just returned.
"Rebecca, do you have the sword? Are you ok?"
"Yes, I'm fine, and I do have the sword."
"We'll be right over."

--and the end is just the beginning--

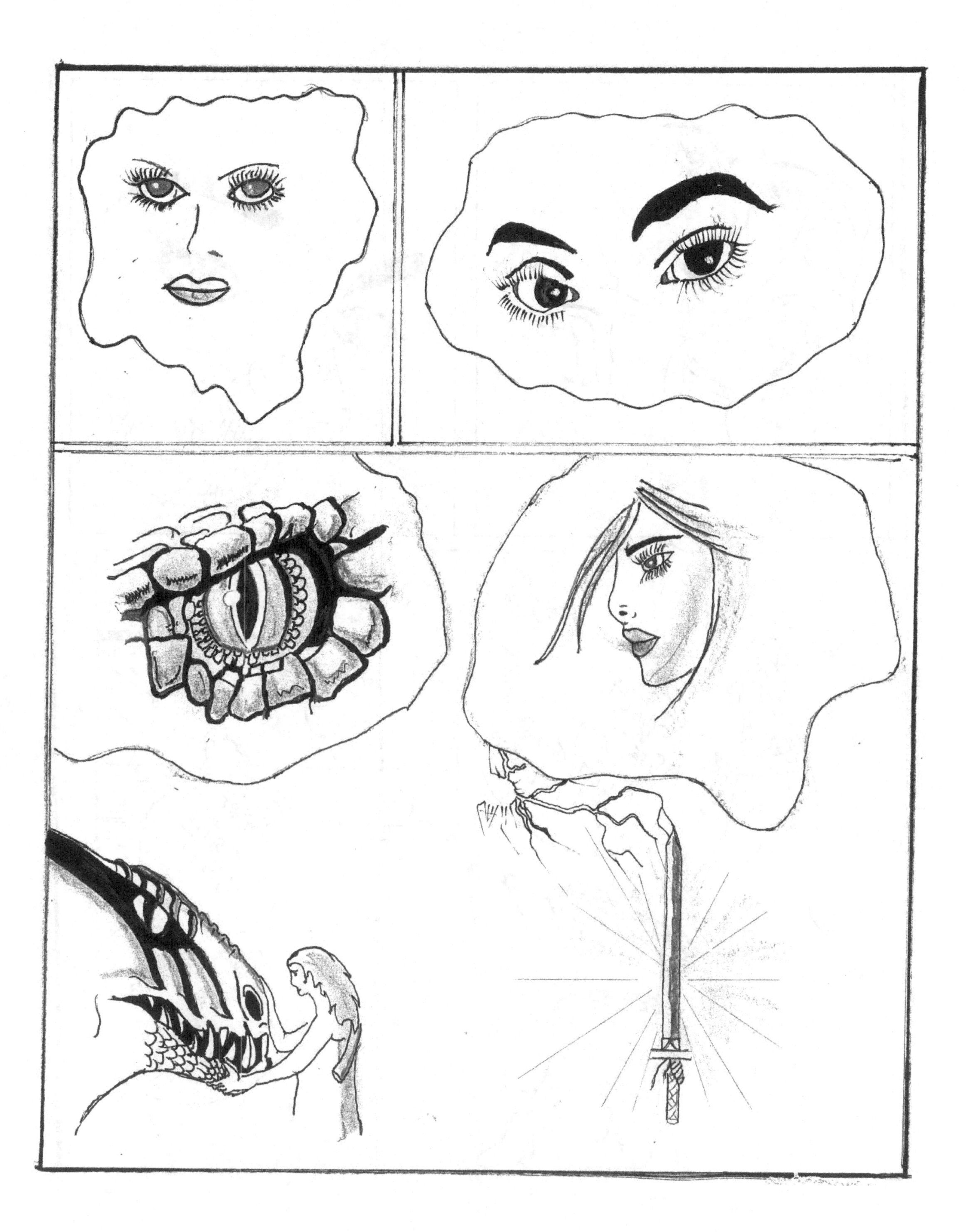

WHAT HAPPEN TO are you O.K.?
lets go Kids
Going to SEE Drag-gon A Very Good Friend of mine
Were ready Mom!
Where we going?
O.K.!
Sniper across the Street
If I Play this right I can get out of this!

I just Want the Sword Mrs Marshall
O.K.
Kassondra Knows What She needs to do next....
Come and get it
Every One Fire!

Printed in the United States
By Bookmasters